THE KID FROM LINCOLN COUNTY

THE KID FROM LINCOLN COUNTY

NELSON NYE

THORNDIKE
CHIVERS

This Large Print edition is published by Thorndike Press, Waterville, Maine, USA and by BBC Audiobooks Ltd, Bath, England.

Thorndike Press is an imprint of Thomson Gale, a part of The Thomson Corporation.

Thorndike is a trademark and used herein under license.

The text of this Large Print edition is unabridged.

Other aspects of the book may vary from the original edition.

Set in 16 pt. Plantin.

LIBRARY OF CONGRESS CATALOGING-IN-PUBLICATION DATA

Nye, Nelson C. (Nelson Coral), 1907–
   The Kid from Lincoln County / by Nelson Nye.
     p. cm.
   ISBN-13: 978-0-7862-9556-2 (alk. paper)
   ISBN-10: 0-7862-9556-2 (alk. paper)
   1. Large type books. I. Title.
PS3527.Y33K53 2007
813'.54—dc22   2007005603

BRITISH LIBRARY CATALOGUING-IN-PUBLICATION DATA AVAILABLE

Published in 2007 in the U.S. by arrangement with
Golden West Literary Agency.
Published in 2007 in the U.K. by arrangement with
Golden West Literary Agency.

U.K. Hardcover: 978 1 405 64152 4 (Chivers Large Print)
U.K. Softcover: 978 1 405 64153 1 (Camden Large Print)

Printed in the United States of America on permanent paper
10 9 8 7 6 5 4 3 2 1

THE KID FROM LINCOLN COUNTY

I

Coming out of the hills and their smell of high pines with the ache of long travel ground into my bones, I sat with both hands shoved against the flat horn and took my first look at Post Oak's single street.

A teeming place — no doubt about it, and hard to believe I was still in Arizona. But this was what gold, and the lust for it, could do. Like an epidemic, I thought, staring down at it; a fine situation to sheer away from if a man set much value on longevity or good health. This, anyway, was Tucson's view of it, the folks I had talked with being angrily vehement, some few plumb aghast or sardonically amused that a button of my tender years and frail appearance would even consider putting out for such a hole.

I had my reasons. And here I was, peering down at the place through the night's blue-black gloom, hearing the hellish sounds lunging up like prodded beasts wild to rip

7

and tear.

Lamplight gleamed from half a hundred gashes, doorslits and windows, spilling out across the yellow dust and the turmoil that churned like something festering there. Fiddle screech clawed above the lift of voices, skreak and rumble of passing wagons, shouts and curses and E-string laughter, the flurry of shots and the tin-panny thump of a tired old piano.

Clint Farris is my handle. Five foot eight and will be seventeen time the cattle crowd get their fall roundup over. No kith nor kin. Far back as I can remember I been doing a man's work — not a proud man's, mind — just the bastardly jobs no one else could be hired for. Missouri and Texas, the Indian Nations. Fort Sumner and Tubac — by God I had a bellyful.

I put the bay gelding down the rough trail and into the press of that traffic-crammed gulch where Post Oak sat on its haunches and howled. The noise and the stinks were near overpowering. As I passed the front of a place labeled GUNSMITH, three gents packing shotguns busted out of an alley and got promptly cut off by a six-mule hitch on a loaded ore wagon. The guy they were after, a frock-coated galoot with a gory knife in his fist, ducked panting between two hard-faced riders and disappeared between the batwings of a nearby saloon. Five frolicking cowprodders burst from another, whooping and yelling fit to wake the dead; one of them, jerking a sixgun, fired five times straight over his head. The shotgun toters swung about and tromped back.

There were more saloons and gambling establishments, from what I could see, than there was anything else. The street was a riot of color and movement. Oil flares orangely painted the dives' high fronts and spilled smoky light across the hawk-faced spielers bull-throatedly barking their wares and incitements. Just across, to the left, was a rambling structure of whipsawed pine which looked and smelled like a honky-tonk. Drawed across its wabbly-topped front were the words BOLL WEEVIL BAR — JEFF DAYNE, PROP. Two barkers out front in tails and silk tiles were reciting the blandishments of the goodies and games.

The walks were so jammed quite a jostle of humanity had taken to the street, adding their blasphemies to the raucous shouts and popping blacksnakes of irate drivers. I had never got into such a racketing confusion. And then, compounding it, a passel of pistol-banging riders came whooping and yipping into town from behind me. They were spread six abreast and taking everything with them, walkers, stray riders — even two rigs filled with giggly females in curly-feathered hats. Off to the right of me eight tied horses snapped a rail from its uprights and tore off like a twister, people diving right and left to get out of the way of that murderous rack.

I backed my horse up on the arcaded walk and let the fools slosh by.

"Damnfool punchers!" some feller beside me growled.

"Punchers, hell!" another exploded. "Them's —" Right there he spotted me and let the rest of it go, fading hastily from sight behind a pair of green batwings.

Kneeing my gelding back into the untangling traffic I said to a head-shaking frock-coated horsebacker, "What outfit was that?"

"Mark Harra's boys; caution, ain't they?"

I said, "What's a man do in this town when he's hungry?"

"You might try the Four Flowers — that's it up ahead."

The grub cost me twice what it was worth, but it filled me. Then, just as I was leaving, I heard a couple of fellers talking about a stage that had been stopped some place between here and Tucson, the bandits getting away with a chestful of silver. "No trouble figurin' who's back of that!" growled one, and his companion nodded.

Going back to the street I climbed into my saddle. Plenty of food for thought around here, impressions too strong to be casually rid of — like the law, for one, being crooked or helpless. And this Harra. Who was he that his men rode roughshod through the town? That bunch had been wearing range clothes but they hadn't much looked like any cowhands I'd known.

I slanched another probing squint up and down the noisy street, weighing the never-still patterns of light and shadow, listening, watching the faces of some of the louder talkers, the ore wagons rumbling through gray ribbons of dust. What I was hunting was a place to put up at.

Neck reining the bay between two rigs, barely clearing a wagon high-sided with lumber so freshly milled you could smell the sap, I pushed the horse toward a sign that said DROVERS INN.

A careening stage jolted past as I rounded two laughing riders. I got down by the steps, dropping the reins across a tie rack. Tramping the porch I went in, abruptly coming to a stop.

It was plain right off I had walked into something. The loutish grins on the faces of the pair by the desk swivelled my glance to the sorrel-top furiously struggling to break the grip of the galoot who had hold of her. It was a foolish thing I did then — I couldn't help it. "Ma'am," I said, "is that whippoor-will botherin' you?"

The feller twisted his neck, showing a hard, scowling mug. "G'on, beat it!" he growled, and went on with his fun.

It was that, I suppose, this contempt, that set me off. I could feel the dark heat coming up through my sinews. With never a thought in that gust of wild hate I caught up a chair and brought it down across his shoulders and, as the girl sprang clear, I hit him with the rest of it. The hinges of his legs let go. He struck the floor all spraddled out.

Still holding the broken back of the chair I considered bare-lipped the pair by the desk. Their jaws hung down; they couldn't believe it. "You boys," I said, "want to buy into this?"

Their grins had departed. One licked his lips, gray-cheeked, shook his head. The other one, though, had more spunk. He was fixing, I reckoned, to claw for his gun handle. I flung what was left of the chair at his face.

He threw up a hand, flexed his knees and

12

got under it. But it cost him the deal. Next thing he saw was the snout of my shooter looking right down his windpipe.

I said: "Well?"

He hung there a moment, stiff and scared, with his cheeks like old putty. I had him cold, and you could see that he knew it. He was mad sure enough, but he wasn't plumb crazy. He fetched both hands over his galluses and uncomfortably swallowed.

"All right," I said. "Get out of them gunbelts. Toss them on the desk — that's right, *careful.* Now get away from them."

A groan came out of the guy on the floor. I moved over far enough to kick the shooter out of his holster. "All right. Get him out of here, and don't come back."

Pretty sullen they looked but didn't shoot off their mouths none. The guy on the floor, the one who'd had hold of the girl, was a long, dark-faced jasper. They got him onto his feet, an arm over each of them. His eyes fluttered open, pale as a snake's. "That's right," I said, "take a *good* look, mister."

He never opened his mouth. Still holding him up, the blood darkly smeared across his cut cheek, they went out.

One thing was for sure, they wouldn't none of them forget this.

■ ■ ■ ■

The girl's sorrel hair was tumbled down around her shoulders. Through that bodeful quiet I heard the breath she sucked in, felt her stare taking hold of me. "You oughtn't to have done that."

Her eyes looked big as walnuts. "I don't mean to sound ungrateful, it's just that. . . ." She looked away, then back. I saw despair in her eyes. "It's just going to make more trouble, and —"

"Trouble," I said, "is a two-way street."

"Not in this town, stranger. That was Geet you knocked down, Harra's wagon boss." She talked like that was pretty near the worst thing. She was mighty upset, the whole look of her darkening. "They'll be laying for you."

"This Harra," I said, "must be a pretty big switch."

She just kept looking at me, nervous, the worries pushing hard at her. Her eyes were a brown that was almost gold. She wasn't my idea of pretty: her nose was turned up, the mouth of her too wide, and she was freckled like a spotted pup. She didn't look old as I was even. Now her cheeks fired up and I flapped into talk, asking what chance

14

there was of getting put up.

"You better climb on a horse and tear out of here!"

She was blunt, all right, if she wasn't nothing else. Matter of fact, it was what I wanted to do; I got hot just wondering if it showed that plain. I managed to dredge up a grin.

She said, "You poor darn fool! You think they're going to let this drop? They'll bury you, boy — that's what they'll do! There ain't a more revengeful skunk in this town than that gun-crazy Geet . . . unless it's Mark Harra." She got powerful earnest. "You jump in your saddle and light a shuck out of here!"

I picked up Geet's pistol and put it by the trappings of them others on the desk. I was scairt, all right. I could see better than her most of the things probably getting chalked up for my future; I ached to fling myself in that saddle. But I knew from experience it wasn't the answer. I said: "About that room —" and she glared, exasperated.

"Can't you see that your staying will only make things worse?" She clenched her fists. "I know these people!"

I knew them, too; at least, their kind. They'd work me over if they ever got the chance; it was the least they would do. Being a orphan, and puny seeming, I'd been

15

pushed around aplenty and was fed to the gills with it. It was time I found out if I was man or mouse. I'd took a stand at last. I'd be done if I run now.

Her eyes bored into me. "I don't want your death on my conscience!"

"That's a pretty hairy kind of talk. You treat all your customers to that sort of gab you won't be long in business, ma'am."

I thought for a minute she was going to bawl, then her look got fierce. She spun away with a snort, and went back of the desk putting up her hair. "It's your life, I guess." Her tone said *Go ahead and get yourself killed.* She made quite a show of consulting the book. "Only room I've got vacant will have to be scrubbed. Scanlon's room — they only just got him out of it." She pushed the guns out of her way and shoved the register around. "You'll have to sign." Her look slanched up. "Better write down some place where your belongin's can be sent."

"Ma'am, you're like to beat that dog plumb to death! All I've got is a horse outside and the clothes on my back."

She said with a sniff, "Just another dumb drifter!"

"Ex-drifter, ma'am. Don't work so hard at it. I'll be gone quick enough if you've called the turn." I bent over and wrote with a flourish *Clint Farris,* then printed after it *Saint Jo, Missouri.*

"The charge is five dollars a night, Mister Farris." She looked at me stubbornly. "I'll be wanting it in advance."

I counted out ten dollars. She said, picking it up, "I hope you know what you're doing," and tucked the bills into the bosom of her blouse, dropping the two cartwheels into a drawer. "You may be tough as a white oak post — for your own sake, Farris, I hope you are, but don't bank too high on it. There've been six gents killed in this town since morning. We buried three yesterday and two the day before. Have you eaten?"

I nodded.

"You can put your horse, if you're bound to stay, in the corral out back, or take him around to Doane's livery." She fussed with her pile of red hair some more. "You want to get up any special time, case you're still, come mornin', among the hearing?"

I allowed there was nothing special about me, that I'd get up when I woke up.

"Your room's thirteen, at the top of the stairs. I'll try to get at it while you're beddin' down your horse."

"Don't you have no help? I mean," I gulped, seeing the wild look she give me, "a

17

place big as this . . . I know it's none of my business. It just sort of struck —"

"You spoke the right word there," she cut in, eyes turning hard. "I guess you're tryin' to be kind, but I don't want your help. I got troubles enough. You look like a Texican! My Dad come out of that country, Farris, and all he ever brung home was grief. Why don't you get out of here?"

That last pretty near was a wail, way she said it. Sure fetched me up short. "Your father's dead?"

"What else would you expect of a man fool enough to stand up to Harra? They rubbed him out the night they took over his Aravaipa claims!"

A voice, while I was staring, coolly said from the door, "You must learn, my dear, to state these truths less ambiguously. It's loose talk of this sort that's behind all these shootings."

II

Graveyards is full of impulsive gents.

Like a possum I hunkered for perhaps half a minute, letting the sound of those words slide through my noggin, while the sorrel-top's cheeks brightly stiffened with anger.

His tone of reproach was a masterful show of tolerance sharp-pulled over the bones of danger. When my look finally swiveled to where he showed it was more of the same, Prince Albert coat and Ascot tie, wolf's grin back of that pussycat smile.

"Who's this?" he said, like turning over a rock.

"Some guy from Missouri, name of Clint Farris." Though her look was stony she seemed cool enough now. "Farris, meet the mayor of Post Oak, Mark Harra."

He was a spare six-footer with a fluff of goat's whiskers sprouting out of his chin. Never bothered to shake my fist. I gave him back his curt nod, watched his glance take me in from busted boots to brush-clawed shirt and sweat-stained hat.

"You figure to be around here long?"

"Hard to say." Then I caught myself, not wanting to seem cagey. "Be gone mighty quick if I can't rustle up a job."

He kept peering at me, bright as a tack. "You the feller hung those scabs on that gunfighter?"

"Well," I said, getting set for trouble, "some of them, I reckon — if you're meanin' Geet — could be chalked up to me." Then, feeling pushed, "You got a ordinance against it?"

He astonished me by chuckling. Amusement winked from his look at the girl. "Where'd you find this sport?" His eyes, dancing back, didn't wait for an answer. "You done just right; that rascal's needed taking down." Now his glance kind of sharpened. "Ever ride shotgun?"

"Maybe you better make that plainer."

Harra grinned. "That's what I like about you. We got a good camp here. Might not hold a patch to Deadwood, but plenty of color if a man can get it out. That's the joker, Farris, getting it out.

"Nearest smelter's over to Galeyville, where that Curly Bill and his bunch hangs out. We've had to come to terms with them buggers — shoved our cost up considerable. Can't say we're rich but we were doing pretty fair till these mask-and-gun guys come meanderin' in."

He steepled his fingers, set a hip against the desk. "Some of the smaller operations have had to close down. A few have sold out, disgusted. Guess we'll all be shutting down pretty soon if we don't find some way around these road agents."

"You mean," I stared, "they're making off with the *ore?*"

"No, they let that through. Nearest bank, though, is Tucson. Miners have to be paid. Don't want ore or promises; they want the cash in their fists. We can't get enough through to chink the ribs of a sandflea." He scowled reflectively and twiddled his watch fob.

"Don't you get checks from the smelter?"

"We get drafts on their account with Lord & Williams, merchants at Tucson. Cash for our payrolls comes up from them — anyway, they ship it."

"How?"

"That part don't seem to make much difference," Harra said, look fiercening. "Whether it comes by stage, private carrier or what, damn little gets past the guns of these vultures."

"That's why you keep guys like Geet in your string?"

"Part of the reason." He didn't say what the rest was.

I said, "There must be a leak."

"Tucson end's as tight as a drum. If the others boys dealt with L & W there might be cause to figure something like that. Only two of us does. Crench, Bloch and Phipstadt do business with the Jacob Brothers' Pima County Bank. The others ship in through a variety of carriers, horseback, and wagon — Sullivan tried getting it in once by mule pack. These buggers stop everything."

"They didn't stop me."

He looked at me sharply, tugged his goatee. The girl went off someplace and he said after a moment, "I tried putting some of my boys on the stage. On dry runs they got by. Last Thursday they brought up a load of cash. Lost it not two miles west of town."

"Looks like the insurance people would —"

Harra snorted. "We can't *get* insurance. Companies won't risk it. Every cent we lose comes straight out of our pockets!" He got his hip off the desk and moved around like a deer fly. Seventh time past he clapped on the brakes. "How'd you like to go to work for me?"

It was the one thing I hadn't looked for him to ask.

"I dunno," I said, wishing the girl would come back. "What'll I take for pay with no cash comin' through?"

Harra's stare banged into my face. "I can scrape up enough for that!" he said.

"What about this Geet? Think he'll cotton to it?"

"He'll stay at heel," Harra said. He stood with both hands deep-shoved in his pockets.

"But why me?" I said. "You don't know me from Adam!"

"Bunch that's grabbing these payrolls don't, either. Look," he growled, "I'll go a hundred a trip! Win, lose or draw. And every time you come through without losing it, Farris, I'll match it with another by way of a bonus! Can't beat that, can you?"

My thoughts juned around like a hatful of hoppers. I thought of them gunfighters swaggering through town, what the girl had said about her old man; but with pay like that I could pile up a stake. It was powerful tempting.

I looked around the dingy lobby, back through the memories of all the gut-chewing yesterdays, at the things I had done — the whacks and crap I had taken just to keep myself from starving. I said: "Who-all will have to know about this — the times, the route an' method?"

"Fix that up anyway you want. I don't care when or how, long as it's soon and we get some cash through."

I peered at the eyes and them bony gray brows set squarely above them, and sucked a breath deep into me. "All right. I'll take a run at it."

"Good boy!" Harra said, and popped out his watch. "How soon can you start?"

"I'll put some thought on it directly."

He eyed the watch again, then put it away. "Might be smart if we kept this just between the two of us. If it should happen to get around you could get yourself killed."

"If it leaks," I growled, "I'll know who to blame. Just keep that Geet jigger off my back."

A door shut someplace. A thump of heels came toward us. Harra said, "You're right," with a great deal of firmness. "This camp won't be safe for women and kids till the most of these thieving rogues have been hanged. I'll do all *I* can toward it."

The girl came in with a bucket and mop. She glanced at him unreadably and went behind the desk. I guessed his last remarks

24

had been chucked out for her. Now he said, "What Post Oak needs is a vigilance committee, something that will put the fear of God into these ruffians. It was the Lord that steered me onto this gold and with His help and guidance I shall run this riffraff hell, west and crooked."

"Well, more power to you," I said, beginning to wonder if he was some kind of a nut.

"It's time," Harra said, "to test the souls of men. I'd be remiss in my duty if I was content to sit by and see these thugs take over. This camp is at the crossroads; if we don't want it made into another Gomorrah every God-fearing Christian has got to take a stand — isn't that so, Miss Quail?"

"It's gettin' pretty fierce," she said.

"Well, a better work awaits my doing," Harra growled. "You think about what I've said, young feller. When the trumpet of the Lord is blown I hope you'll be on the right shore, brother."

The Quail girl didn't take long, once he'd gone, to show what that talk had done for me. "Well!" she said, the sound of it matching the curl of her lip, "I can see no one needs to fret and stew about you!"

I said, halfway graveled, "Don't go grabbin' up the pepper."

Her chin came out about a foot and forty inches. "You . . . you *carpetbagger,* you! To think," she cried in that withering voice, "I was fool enough to —" With a sniff of disgust she let the rest of it go. "Go on. Get out."

"Now see here! I paid for a room in this place."

"And I figured *you* for a Texas man. Texas!" she said with her eyes bright as glass. She sloshed up a shotgun standing back of the desk, snatched the bills from her blouse and flung them at me. "Git!"

"But, ma'am —"

"If you want to hitch up with that kind of varmint you sure ain't about to stay here, Clint Farris. Hit a lope! Start making tracks or sure as my name's Heidi Quail, by godfries, I'll blast you into the middle of next week!"

Outside, pushing through some red-shirted Cousin Jacks clomping up the steps, I'd got as far as the bottom, looking for a chance to cross the walk, when something I saw at the hitch pole drove the last gasp of tolerance out of me. A sharp faced galoot in a green-and-black striped shirt was picking my gelding's reins off the rack.

26

I gathered myself. "Get away from that horse!"

Something tugged at my sleeve. I heard the bang of a shot. That walk cleared like a stampede had gone over it, folks jumping every whichways. I got a fist on my shooter as a second clap nearly snatched the hat from my head. Clouting the brim off my nose I slapped a slug toward the flash.

Somebody screamed. Some guy called "Damn!" The horse rustling party in the green-and-black shirt got an arm across the saddle and tried to cork me with a quick one. I ducked and whirled left, was trying to get him in my sights when someone grabbed my shoulder and spun me clear around.

"Drop that," this jasper said, "or I'll blow —"

That far he got. My fist went *splat* against the side of his jaw. It knocked him reeling across the planks and into the yellow dust of the road; and just as he went flopping I saw the glint of the star on his vest.

III

Looked like the smartest thing I could do was pile into leather and cut a streak for the tules. It was a powerful fine notion and, regardless of temper, I would probably have done it except that ranny in the two-colored shirt already had wropped himself around my saddle and was pounding a hole through the wind with my bronc.

I still had hold of the gun, but what with the dust and all them people I hadn't a Junebug's chance of connecting. Putting it away I went over to the badge packer.

He was a small wiry gent with a face like boiled leather. He was up on one elbow, groaning, glaring, trying to get the legs under him. Despite his hard luck he seemed to look pretty capable as I got him onto his feet, brushed him off and found his hat. He had a mort of restraint — I got to hand him that. Some of the gab going round wasn't learned at no woman's knee, and not a few of this bunch that was licking their chops appeared the kind that would enjoy watching somebody get the bejazus knocked out of them.

He didn't say much straightoff, but stood looking me over with them elk colored eyes, opening and shutting the bottom half of his face like to maybe find out how much that jaw was still good for. "Don't believe I caught your name," he said finally.

"Clint Farris," I told him. "I'm pretty new around here."

"Have eye trouble, do you?"

His tone got sharper. "You make it a habit to go round beltin' marshals?"

"Sorry about that. Never noticed the badge till after I'd conked you," I said, knowing he was riled and thinking probably he had some right to be. "I was kind of excited."

"Anything wrong with your hearin'?"

"Now, look," I said, with the rage clawing up again, "I told you I was sorry!"

"You had a gun in your fist. *I* told you to *drop* it."

It wasn't only this. All the times I'd been pushed around other places got to churning and squirming and clouding my judgment. I kept trying to stay cool, trying to see this guy's side, but I could feel it piling up. In that bunch crowding round there was grins and eager looks enough to let me know this could be damn rough if a man wasn't careful.

"All right," I said. "If you hadn't grabbed hold I might have used better sense. I didn't stop to think — but who the hell would when he's watchin' some jasper getting set to lift his horse!"

The marshal heard me out then looked around, presently saying, "You don't seem to have much support for that statement, Farris. What kind of horse was it?"

"A bay gelding," I told him, "with a beat-up Hamley saddle," but only one of the bunch around us gave in to having seen such an outfit, and he wouldn't own to being positive about it. Another said, "Longly, I wouldn't be surprised if this whole thing wasn't hogwash," and three — four hard-faced watchers nodded.

Longly, it appeared, was the marshal's name. He said, "What sort of lookin' jigger was this feller you claim took your horse? Fat, skinny, tall or short?"

"About average, I reckon. Face like a hatchet."

"You really *see* this guy?"

I guess some of the heat that juned up in me showed. While I was trying to get on top of my temper he said like he figured the whole deal was plain bunk, "Let's see your bill of sale for that nag."

I didn't fish through my pockets because I'd nothing to fish for. I'd swapped a roan filly for that bay about six months ago in the Indian Nations, never thinking to have my right to him questioned. I told the marshal I didn't have one. He scowled a while and gruffly asked what brand the horse was packing.

"Never had no brand," I said, feeling trapped, "but the guy that took him had on a green-and-black shirt with pearl buttons."

I can't say why, but I got the notion it was about the worst thing I could have told this gazebo. He'd been scowling already; now his face sucked in around the shape of his teeth and it looked for a minute like he was going to lay hands on me. I saw mouths flop open and grinners grinned fiercer, but all that flint-eyed badge packer said was, "Farris, don't be around here come mornin'."

I thought of several things I might of said to him, but time I latched onto them he'd got the traffic going and was dragging his spurs up the other walk. The crowd had broke up. But some gents was still around, with a hereafter shine about the way they stood watching. Sweat began to crack through my pores. I chucked myself between a pair of bat-wings, burrowed up to a bar and dropped some money on a beer.

It wasn't much cooler than the planks outside, but it was wet.

Some frail in a short skirt joggled my elbow. Half sliding off the white of her shoulders was this peekaboo deal of some thin colored fluff you could of put pea soup through and never lost a drop. Blue-black hair piled against a red comb, a full mouth of teeth bared now in a grin with a kind of secret-feeling oozing out of that look that told me plain I had better get lost because, in spite of them duds, there was something damn queer. No paint on her cheeks, and things bulging out of that jumpity stare so laced with panic you could mighty near taste it.

I had come to this camp hunting greener pastures but this was a little too green for me. Gripped by confusion I was shaking, plumb edgy. Any fool would of known that was coffin bait, yet I swiveled my ears for another quick squint.

I saw him then. Big as a blowed-up toad and gray. Shoe-button eyes in the shaved-hog scowl of a three-chinned face that was livid with fury as he whipped out a knife and come to his feet. It wasn't clear who he planned to skewer — her or me — nor I wasn't about to wait around to find out.

I sure wasn't hankering to be no dead hero.

When his arm went back I went over the bar. I lit spraddled out, came off the floor full of fright and spied this apron coming for me with a bung-starter. I swept up a bottle, let him have it in the gut. As he went down I saw a door. With a gasp I had it open. Something tore it out of my hand but, crouching low, I flung myself through into a dark that was blacker than the scairt dame's hair.

What with all the racket and the heart barging in me like a battery of stamps, I wasn't too cool and optimistic myself. I'd got into a storeroom — this much I could tell by the sourish stink. Some light splashed in from that open door, but before my sight could begin to take hold my ears picked up a thump of running boots. With both arms out in front of me like feelers I skittered around maybe eight or ten barrels and come head-on into a wall of stacked crates.

Bottled goods. I reckoned it was pretty near time I was digging up something that might slow them down a little.

I could have chopped out a tune on my shooter, but seemed like there had ought to be something less drastic I could do to improve things. When the crates began to sway I knew I'd found it. I reached the end of the line, ducked behind and crouched there, trying to keep the breath from whistling through my teeth.

The clatter of boots got louder and quit. I knew they were standing there, peering and listening, waiting for me to give them a cue. I mighty near done it. A floorboard skreaked with the shift of weight, and, not fiddling for nothing, I put both arms against them crates and shoved.

The whole works toppled with a hell of a crash.

Just back of me now was the dockside door. I flung up the bar and dived through with the guns and shouts beating up a wild clamor. I didn't say no goodbyes. I hit the ground running and plunged into the night.

Like the marks set into a tally book all the things I had done in this camp came slithering back one by one through my confusion to beset and confound me. Every reflex, each habit cravenly endorsed to duck trouble, stared aghast at such audacious tomfoolery. How could I have been so incredibly stupid!

These were my thoughts, my silent shivering companions of the interminable eternity I crouched beneath that honky-tonk dock waiting for the hubbub I had loosed to quiet down.

Never in all my life had I so much as even laid hands on a man, not before I had come to Post Oak. Sure I'd been tired of it, fed to the gills with inching round like a cat-watched mouse, cursed, cuffed and spat at like some broken-down swamper in a river-mouth tavern. But it had kept me alive.

When a guy gets orphaned at no older than eight, staying alive can get to seem mighty important. That kind of figuring can surely take hold of you to where, pretty soon, a man will put up with anything.

Still —

I wasn't sure now I'd not been right in the first place. Oh, I'd felt pretty fine swapping gab with Mark Harra, making out to be someone he could afford to spend time with. Now I was scairt even to recollect such craziness — me, riding shotgun to a fortune in specie! The meek might never inherit the earth but at least they were part of the observable community.

It's the inconspicuous ones that stay longest, the ordinary Joes no one takes a second look at. The forgotten people. Their name is legion. I'd have traded every hope I had of the hereafter to slip back again into that hated obscurity — and don't think I wasn't thinking about it.

The forgotten people — how pleasant they seemed, those inconspicuous ones, but the worm had turned too far for that. There was too many now had seen and heard. That scairt dame upstairs. That triple-chinned tub with the Arkansas toothpick — they wouldn't forget me. Or Mark Harra, or Geet that I'd broken the Quail girl's chair over, or that horse-grabbing weasel in the green-and-black shirt! I hadn't even the means of skinning out of this burg, just them eight paper dollars and maybe a handful of change. Might buy a stage seat, but would they let me climb into it?

It was quiet out there beyond the dock's edge now. Peering into that dark my tongue was dry as the flowers put away between the pages of a Bible. More I stared the more reluctant I was to move even a finger.

My legs was cramping. I knew I had to crawl out, get some place where I could comb a little sense from the muddle of confusion juning round inside my noggin. I could hear the far sounds of turning wheels and horse hoofs, fiddle scrape and tavern noise, but the blackness of this alley lay as still as a gut-shot gopher.

There'd be trash underfoot but the best chance I thought would be to sashay along the dark backs of these buildings, and that was what I did. For as far as I was able. But, stumbling along through the heaved-out junk, I came all too soon to a point so choked with broken crates and splintered boxes I couldn't see no way of getting past without a racket. The gulch wall had pinched in and was too rock-studded and steep for tackling. I could sense this much.

I began to sweat, not wanting to go back, not at all anxious either to wade around in that stack of kindling. I couldn't even see how far it went; and, while I was staring, trying to make up my mind, something slapped against wood like a scrabbling of claws. A door hinge skreaked. Labored, panting breaths spilled out of a slather of struggling shapes, a heavier black against the door's open hole. I couldn't wiggle a toe until, out of a grumbled mumble of cursing, sheared the jumpity climb of a woman's thin screams.

My eyes pawed them then. It was too late to run, and no place to dash for without I could barrel past into that room — but they were too near for that. Grabbing out my shooter I looked for a head to hit, but this mealy gloom was thicker than porridge and the way they were swirling there was too much chance of clobbering the girl.

While I was hopping from one foot to the other some cluck in the next shack threw up a shade, light from that window pouring into the alley. This pepperneck yelled, "What're you damn fools tryin' to do!"

I never wasted the twist of my jaw on him. Every thinking fiber of me was clapped like my stare to the stamp and sway of that pair of locked shapes, to the two-colored arm wedged beneath the girl's chin, black and green in a grip that was choking her life out.

I lit into him with my gun-weighted fist, busting to see the blood spurt. I didn't care about the girl. With the fury swelling through me I had eyes for only the damned chisel face of that horse-thieving son who had left me afoot. His arms slashed out. Shaken loose of the girl he went reeling back in a clatter of rowels. Before he could drop I tied into him again, clouting him hard across the throat with my pistol. He went down like a dog that's had the wind kicked out of him.

I was wild enough to finish him, but the girl dragged me off.

"Quick!" she cried, and I could feel the pant of her breath on my cheek, the frantic need in that cry getting through to me finally. "We've got to get out of here!"

That nump from next door was still yelling his brains out, but the sharp urgent edge to her words fetched my face around. "You!" I growled, and got stiffly up, hearing the thump of hurrying boots.

She was pulling the ends of her torn blouse together; and this wasn't the frail which had triggered the rage of that knife waving slob in the Boll Weevil either. This was Heidi Quail, the sorrel-haired Harra hater — her of the Texas temper that, because I'd seen fit to swap gab with the mayor, had refused me a room I had already paid for and driven me at gunpoint into the street.

I took another hard look at the guy on the ground, a hatchet-faced rat if I ever had seen one. A couple more cuffs with the barrel of a pistol and he would be about ready to cough up my gelding. I started for him again but the girl spun me round.

"Ain't you done enough now?" She tugged impatiently. "Come on hit a lope."

"Hold up!" someone snarled. But, stumbling and cussing, she yanked me along through that tangle of crates with no regard for the shouts that was churning up back of us. A pair of slugs whistled past as we dived into the dark. It was just beginning to look like we'd make it when a wide-shouldered shape speared up out of the gloom and a gun's bore dug into the wince of my belly.

"That's about far enough!" a tight voice said maliciously; and there was other dark shapes piled up solid behind him. I shoved both fists high above my ears. "All right, Geet," this guy said, "fetch the lantern."

IV

Boiling under my breath, I knew one thing for sure: If I got out of this bind you could dunk me in bean sprouts and call me "Chink" if I ever lined up on the short side again.

The guy with his gun in my gut was the marshal, Jim Longly. "So it's you again, Farris!" There was a hard satisfaction a-tramp in his tone. "We'll step along to my office." He slanched a look at the girl. "I guess you better come with us."

He motioned with the pistol and the crowd opened up, Geet striding ahead into the street with his lantern.

"What's the charge?" I asked, trying to uncover some hole. When nobody bothered to give me a hand I recollected the advice this great seizer had given me right after I'd got done brushing him off. It wasn't all I remembered. There was the matter of that chair I'd busted over Geet's head, and the guy in the Boll Weevil I'd smacked with the bottle. They wouldn't have much trouble working up a charge. Least I could expect was a couple of weeks in the Post Oak pokey.

A lather of thinking rampaged through my noggin, none of it calculated to bolster my hopes much, but there was no point getting the girl dragged into it. I told Longly so. I said, "She don't know me from Adam."

Began to seem like these jaspers was all deaf as gateposts.

When we got to the jail, Geet with his lantern, went up the steps first, then the girl still holding her blouse pulled together. Be a fine pass if they claimed I'd put hands on *her!*

I swabbed some of the sweat off the back of my neck. The marshal's eyes shooed me after them and it sure didn't seem like I had much choice. In all that bunch of staring faces I couldn't find one that held any encouragement. My shooter was in his pocket and the one in his fist was peering right at me. I sucked in a fresh breath and went reluctantly up, hearing Longly, behind me, advising the crowd to get on about its business.

He came in, slammed the door, parked a hip on the desk. He said real quiet, "What's it going to be, Farris, — reasonable or pain-ful?"

I allowed I would do my best to co-operate.

"Smart boy," he said, and waved the girl into a chair. "You can start by tellin' us why you killed him."

I looked to see if he was funning. He wasn't. "Hell's fire," I said, "I ain't killed nobody."

The place got so quiet you could hear the clock. Longly finally got off the desk. "That your idea of co-operation, Mac?"

The edges of a frown kind of framed his smile, and it was traipsing across my no-tions we could all come out of this consider-able nicer if we'd made a real effort to stay on top of our tempers. Having lit on this gem I said, to seem hopeful, "If we could sort of come up on the off-side . . . maybe a different approach?"

His eyes stared at me across the fold of his arms while the outside noises sort of drifted away. "All right. You've got to Post Oak. Work it up from there."

I didn't know what to say, hardly.

"What was the first thing you done?" Longly asked, thinly patient.

"Stopped at a hash house. It was just get-tin' dark."

43

Geet said with a sneer, "Then you went to the Boll Weevil?"

"No, that was later." My look skittered off the dark loom of his face. "I figured I had better find some place to put up at."

"So you went to the Drover's," Longly said. "Then what'd you do?"

My mouth felt stiff. This cat-and-mouse deal of ask and answer was running cold chills across the ends of my neck hair. I tried not to notice Geet's plaster-patched cheeks or the brightening shine of his gunbarrel stare. I said, "Harra come in," and saw them swap pleasured glances.

Nobody mentioned my little spree with the chair.

"Well?" Longly said with his tone bland as peach fuzz. "What did he want?"

You could almost see their ears lean out, waiting. I'd be no good to Harra without I kept the most of that stuff to myself. As things stood he looked to be the only hole card I was like to come up with. While I was mulling which way to jump, the Quail girl said, "He dropped by to see me."

It should have taken me off the hook, but you could tell by the quiet how much it had helped. Nobody looked at her. She might better have stayed out of it I thought, watching Geet.

"Having been raised right, not wanting to get in the way of a man's courtin'," Longly chucked at me, obnoxiously polite, "this pilgrim takes himself over to the Boll Weevil. That how it sounds to you, Geet?"

My tongue got dry as a last year's leaf. Harra's gunfighter said with a bully-puss grin, "You want I should loosen him up a little?"

Longly dropped back to rest his rump on the desk, eyeing me like he was giving some thought to it. "In a camp like this a marshal has to learn to budget his time. Now I'm a reasonable man." He tipped his head to one side. "I try to give every guy the best shake I can."

"You've convinced me," I said. "I went over there."

"Now," Geet grinned, "we're gettin' some place. So you got cozy with Dayne and he dug up this deal."

"I never saw no Dane."

"*Jeff* Dayne," he said, like that should mean something to me.

I twisted a glance at the marshal.

"Look," Geet scowled, shoving out his left mit. When my head tipped down that fist flew up like the hoof of a mule.

I woke up in a chair, the whole front of me soaked, water running off my chin and both ears. I couldn't see extra good and the middle of my face felt like it wasn't there no more.

I shook my head and wished I hadn't. When the room quit whirling Harra's gunfighter had me by the front of the shirt. He hauled me out of the chair. I slammed into a wall. I thought, by God, he'd broke the back of my skull.

When I got back enough sense to realize he hadn't, he still had me pinned there like a bug on a board. I was too badly shook to pile much of a mad on, too scairt I'd catch more if I opened my mouth. "You oughta watch where you're goin'," he grinned.

He let go of me when he judged I could stand. Longly, the marshal, said, "Let's start again. This time, Farris, try to be more careful." He gave Geet the nod.

The gunfighter said: "You went over to the honky-tonk. What happened then?"

"I had a beer at the bar."

"You talk to anyone?"

It wasn't easy to think after what I'd been through. My head felt like it was opening and shutting, like bubbles fritterin' up out of a bog and going *plop.* "I don't think so," I said, and saw the nastiness start to come out on his face again. "This dame drifted up —"

"Which dame? What'd she look like?"

"Well, she had black hair pulled back around a comb."

"Verdugo," Longly said. "Go on."

"Anyway, while she was giving me the eye, this hog-fat jasper back among the tables comes out of his chair with a face like thunder. Next thing I know he's got a knife up to throw. I got out of there fast."

I couldn't tell about Longly, but it was plain by Geet's look he wasn't buying any part of it. "You beat a knife?" he said.

"I went over the bar, smacked a apron with a bottle, yanked open a door, got into this place filled with barrels and —"

Longly said, "That's pretty hard to believe."

"Looks like you could check it."

Through the sneer on his puss, Harra's gunfighter said, "Sounds to me he's about ready for Lesson Number Two."

"Let's hear the rest of it," Longly decided.

I told them the truth, even to how I'd ducked under that dock. I said to the plain disbelief on their faces, "When I figured they'd quit looking I moved off down that passage, thinkin' it might fetch me out near enough that, with any kind of luck, I could make it to the Drover's. Somebody jumped out of one of them back doors —"

47

"Yeah," Geet said with his teeth skinned. "To hear this kid o-rate half the town's got it in for him!" The marshal, swinging his leg, observed, "Some guys is like that. Can't hardly get out of bed without splittin' their britches." He pared off a chew and popped it into his jaw. "You got any more questions?"

"Gettin' back to the Drover's," Geet said, "why'd you kill him?"

They had me so jumpy I was scairt to say anything. Longly said, quiet, "It's a fair question. Answer it."

I was sure enough caught between a rock and a hard place. If I told them the truth I would probably get smacked again, and not to say anything would certain be asking for it. If I could have got word to Harra, or fetched him into this someway — but it was plain if I did I'd be worth less than nothing, far as he was concerned. That job he had mentioned was supposed to be kept quiet. "Is there a lawyer in this camp?"

It come out pretty meek but I saw the quick shuffle of looks them two swapped. Longly got his butt off the desk. "He was found in your room, kid. Why don't you own up to it?"

"I ain't *got* no room!"

Longly's eyes fastened to me. "What kind

of talk's that? You just told us you was hopin' to get back there. Your name's in the book. You signed for that room at the top of the stairs."

"Don't tell me you never been in it," Geet said.

He was having more fun than a barrel of monkeys.

"Well, it's true!" I growled — "I never even been up them stairs!"

You'll probably wonder why I kept squirming when it was plain from the start this pair aimed to scuttle me. I suppose hope dies hard when your whole life's ahead of you. You got to recollect I was only seventeen, that I was pretty shook up and that, in spite of my experience, I still thought a marshal was made of better clay than most. When Heidi Quail spoke out to vouch for my contention I dragged in a fresh breath and come away from the wall. I felt free already and was working up a grin when Longly said, looking hard at the girl: "You puttin' in your oar again?"

She got white around the mouth but shoved him back stare for stare. "He never had anything to do with it!" she cried. "Look at him, for heaven's sake — he's *only* a boy!"

"Some rattlers is young, too," Geet

49

sneered, "but you can croak just as sure from them as any others."

"I tell you he never saw the room."

"What is he," Longly said, "some sort of damn fool? Signin' for it, payin' for it —"

"I gave him back his money, told him this camp was no place for a kid."

Longly, staring, said from the side of his mouth: "Frisk him, Geet."

Harra's gunfighter, grinning, fetched something out of my pants and held it up where the both of them could see it. "If you sent him packing," the marshal said, "what's he doing with that key in his pocket?"

V

I seemed to remember her pushing it across the Drover's desk, but that was as far as recollection took me. That gol-rammed Geet was shining up his fist again.

It wasn't clear what connection he might have with the marshal but it was plenty apparent if I didn't talk quick I'd soon be in no kind of condition to. "Is this ape packing tin? Some kind of deputy marshal mebbe?"

"Just a public spirited citizen who happened to be along when I ran into you," Longly scowled.

"Then what about taking a couple of good looks at him? When I first went over there huntin' a room this 'public spirited citizen' just happened to have both paws on this girl and she didn't look like she was enjoyin' it none. She —"

Geet swung. I ducked. The marshal, red-faced, yelled for Geet to back off; and, behind him, Heidi Quail with a hand still gripping her blouse bounced onto her feet like hell getting ready to take off on cart wheels.

Geet, voice filled with protest and bluster, hauled his wide shoulders round to fix Jim Longly with an affronted glare. "You swallerin' that crap?"

The marshal looked at the girl. He seemed a little embarrassed. She said, "Why don't you ask him how he got so banged up?"

"Aw," Geet said, "I told you about that."

The girl said, pinkly furious, "Did he tell you this fellow broke a chair over his head?"

Longly's elk-colored eyes began to look riled. "If you been using my badge —"

"Chrissake!" Geet yelled, "you gonna —"

Longly said sharply, "Either stop that shouting or get out of this office." He was white around the gills and it looked for a bit like Geet, all swelled up, was going to sure enough make tracks. He half wheeled to do it, then got hold of himself. "It wasn't that way at all," he growled, looking misused and sullen. "All I done — hell, I told you about him!"

The marshal peered at me again, and I thought maybe he didn't know what to believe. He sloshed a look at the girl. She pulled her chin up, flushing. She said, hotly scornful, "I always figured, Jim Longly, that you was anyways *honest!* I didn't think being turned down by a girl would warp you into —"

"We're not investigating me," the marshal said stiffly. "Geet claims this feller's a pal of Charley Bowdre, Bill Scroggins and Doc Scurlock — a back-shooting killer, wanted over in Lincoln County. One of the sort, Geet says —"

"Geet says!" she snapped. "He's a fine one to talk about back-shooting killers! You ever think for yourself? Or do all your judgments jump full-grown from the unsupported say-so of Mark Harra's gunslingers?"

Longly, pulled two ways, cried, "That's not fair!" Then, probably reminded they were not alone, he wiped the torn look off his cheeks and swiveled that bitter stare back to me. "I understood, Farris, you come from Texas. Why'd you write 'Saint Jo' in that register?"

Why does a guy do a heap of things? I just scowled and shrugged. But the girl, still riding the blood in her eye, didn't look like she would back off for anything. "I don't know what you're trying to pin on this boy, but I'll swear on a stack of prayerbooks he never once had that thing in his hand!"

It was the second time she had called me 'boy'. I could feel the blood pounding into

53

my head; the marshal and Geet wasn't tickled none, neither. Geet was opening his trap when he said, whirling on him, "Any mean-minded skunk with a key in his fist can make like he's took it out of someone else's pocket!"

"That's a . . . she's just tryin' to git even!" he snarled, turning ugly.

Kind of seemed like Longly was beginning to wake up. Lip on lip like two chunks of granite he peered a mighty time at that squirming polecat. "Even for what?" he said, soft as spiders.

Spluttering, Geet went back a couple of steps. "Why . . . uh, hell, you know dang well she's had it in for Harra's boys! Ever since her ol' man fell down that shaft."

Longly's cheeks was pale as a puff of smoke, them elk-colored eyes of his shining like glass. Geet's look got a little wild, and he swore.

If I had kept still then the whole course of this deal might of took a different turn; but I cried out, just remembering, "Say! That feller back there!"

All their heads swiveled round. I said, obsessed with it, "He's the one got away with my horse, dad-drat him!"

Longly's darkening stare went from me to the girl. "You got any idea what he's jabbering about?"

Heidi shook her head.

I stared like a nump. She looked completely at sea. "That pinch-faced sport in the black an' green shirt," I said, "the one you was wrasslin' with."

That girl wasn't helping me one dang bit. You'd of thought I was ready for a string of spools. The marshal said, "He sounds like his needle's stuck."

The girl glowered back at him. "I think your pal must have scrambled his brains. You ought —"

"But he's back in that alley!" I cut in, bound to have myself heard. Of course I was graveled; who wouldn't be? This seemed like, to me, a chance to get myself cleared of whatever it was they were trying to pile on me, if I could prove I'd been tangling with that son of a buck. "You could anyways look!" I told Longly, fuming.

"I got other fish to fry right now," the marshal said. "We're going over to the Drover's and have a look at that corpse — you, too, Geet. You can lead the way."

In the Drover's tiny lobby the girl pulled up by her desk. "I believe, if you don't mind, I'd just as soon wait here."

The marshal's look was searching. "I

should think you'd want to —"

Heidi Quail shook her head, folding brown arms across the mauled blouse. "To tell you the truth it's getting monotonous. You might as well know I've been seriously considering throwing in with Buck Peters in that coffin and headstone business he's got. Every guy in this camp that's picked to throw in the sponge seems to wind up in this place to get the job done."

"I've noticed that," Longly nodded. "Geet, help Farris navigate them stairs."

We went up to the second floor, the marshal fetching a lamp off the desk. A long hall opened up; to the left and just topping the stairs was a closed door on which, in white chalk, was the number 13. Longly, passing the lamp to the Harra wagon boss — at least that was his job according to Heidi — dug out the key Geet had fished from my pocket. "After you," he growled, and threw open the door.

I followed Geet in. He held up the lamp, watching my expression from the corners of his eyes. He slipped the lamp in a bracket. "I see you know 'im," he said nastily.

"That's dumping considerable weight where it don't rightly fit." I took another squint at the guy on the floor. "I got stopped alongside him on the street — it was when you rode in from wherever you'd been with that bunch of yippin' hooligans. We was crowdin' the walk and I asked how come the whole town ducked for cover. He said you was some of Harra's gun hands."

"What else did he say?" Longly asked from the door. He hadn't hardly been civil since I'd popped it at him to go look at that feller. He hadn't hugged Geet either. He would growl out this talk and scarcely notice what it got him, like there was something gnawing his mind that figured to be of larger importance.

Like now. Never bothering to wait for any answer, he gruffed, "Let's get out of here."

Back in the office it was Geet that took over, Longly appearing satisfied to hunker in the back seat like a chicken with the pip. If this brooding bothered Geet it sure as heck wasn't much apparent. He said with his snoot six inches from mine, "You're stuck with this, kid, so make it easy for yourself. What'd that chump hev on you?"

I couldn't help sighing. "He didn't have a thing."

"Then why'd you kill him?"

"I didn't," I said, and wondered which hand he would take to me.

"He was killed in your room, kid."

"I can't help that. When I went up there

with you was the first time —"

"Kid," he said, "I got that key from your pocket. The marshal seen me, so don't give us that. It's the only key there is to the room."

"Just because you say so don't make it a fact."

He stepped back a bit and held up his fist. "You want me to knock you through that wall?"

"You might's well tell the truth," Longly said. "You saw I had to use the key to get in there."

Before I could find any answer to that the jail office door was flung protestingly open and heavy steps made the floor skreak. Geet's eyes narrowed warily and Longly said irrascibly, "What do you want here, Jeff?"

I jerked one fluttery look and knew I had come against the end of my string. It was the three-chinned jasper who'd sprung up with that knife just before I went over the Boll Weevil's bar.

VI

His shaved-hog face appeared as smooth as
a mill pond. There wasn't a particle of
menace, yet the crackle of frost seemed to
hang in this place plain as cut mistletoe
strung from a rafter. Geet scarcely breathed.
The marshal looked like he'd been caught
in a melon patch.

The faintest tug of a grin twitched the
newcomer's mouth, but nobody appeared
to be finding much fun in it. "What have
you got this kid in here for?"

Longly couldn't get enough spit to talk
with. It was Geet who presently got around
to saying I was being asked some questions
in connection with a killing.

The fat man paid no attention to Geet.
Eyeing the marshal he said: "Some more of
Harra's back-of-the-bush stuff?" His scorn
fired Longly's cheeks. "When are you going
to get onto yourself?"

"One of these times you'll push me too

far!" Longly flared, but the words seemed to carry more bluster than threat. He looked doughy and sick, and he jammed shaking hands in his pockets to hide them.

It wasn't till he took off his steel-rimmed cheaters, blinking near-sightedly as he huffed and polished them on the front of his shirt, it became apparent to me the big guy wore spectacles. I could see the wild thoughts juning through Geet's stare, and the wanting of it tugging him so bad you could taste it, but for all that he stood there like a chunk of stuck machinery.

But the fat man's next words woke me up. "How much bail you holding him on?"

The marshal said with a plain reluctance, "No bail's been set. He ain't been arraigned."

"You mean," said the fat man, hooking on his cheaters for a long, and careful look at me, "Geet hasn't been able to pound a confession out of him?"

"I don't have to take —"

"You'll take it, Jim." The fat man sighed. "Have you got any evidence at all against the boy?"

"I've got enough," Longly glowered. "He put up at the Drover's. 'You Bet' Farley was found croaked in his room. Door was locked an' the key, when we found it, was in the

60

kid's pocket!"

The big guy done some more quiet looking. "Suggestive," he nodded, "but hardly conclusive. Somebody else, one of Harra's hardcases —"

"Guess you ain't heard about them new locks Heidi's put on the doors. Take a special key, and there's only one key given out to each lock, all different. He had the key on him. No one else could have got in."

"How'd you know this dead shyster was in there?"

Geet took to twitching like a tromped-on centipede, but the marshal's stare looked froze in his face. I watched his tongue scratch across dry lips; even then I had to stretch hard to hear him. "In where?" he said, like it had come from his bootstraps.

"In the kid's room. If the door was locked and he had the key with him?"

It took perhaps three seconds for their jaws to fall, and I wasn't no quicker to catch on how marvelous these two barracudas had slammed into the bait, caught with full mouths of the porridge cooked for me.

Geet looked pretty ugly, but what was there to say? This slickery pair had yapped too much already.

The fat guy's cheeks were smooth as a

biscuit but the eyes behind them steel-rimmed cheaters wasn't missing a trick. "Kid, pick up your hat. We're clearing out," he said.

Longly stood there looking sick while I filched my shooter out of his pocket, caught up the hat and dragged my spurs across the floor. The night air was cold as we tromped down the steps, myself turned jumpy as a cart full of crickets, watching him slanchways from the corners of my stare.

In the street he stopped, then faced me square. "You got no cause to be afeared of me, boy. If so be you're a mind to, turn loose of me here; there'll be no hard feelings on my part."

I was tempted, believe me. I could still see the fright in Verdugo's crouch and remember them moments when, by yanking that knife, this smooth-talking walloper had give such a hard time to me in that deadfall.

Nothing I put my thoughts to made sense. I wasn't halfway sure he hadn't fished me out of there to take care of personal. One swipe of that Arkansas toothpick could do it; and them fair words he'd spoke wasn't blinding me none. I'll own up I was anxious, but this seemed like a chance to get a few of the things that was gnawing me answered.

I said, "How come you was trying to hook

that knife in me a while ago?"

"Wasn't *you* I was after," he grumbled, peering about. "Tell you soon's we get off this street." His stare kept picking at the black between buildings, and his voice came out gruffer. "You stringing along?"

"I'll take a samplin'," I said, and stepped after him warily, one hand nervously fisted about the butt of my shooter. I reckon that was childish, set beside everything else, but I still had in mind that last look at Geet, and the burning fury I had seen quivering out of him.

We got into Dayne's bar without no untoward incidents, though the relief of having done it pretty near unstrung me. Some of the custom shoved back to make a place for us at the mahogany. My big friend called for a double shot, said, "Boy, git that inside of you."

I've never drunk nothing that burned like that; I could feel the stuff climbing through every sinew. And while I was gagging, trying to catch my breath, a hand on my arm was moving me confidently into his office. I dropped into a chair. He pulled out a desk drawer to prop booted feet, watching me through the thick shine of his cheaters.

"As you likely have guessed, I'm Jeff Dayne," he said, frowning. He pulled in a

63

deep breath and scrubbed a hand over his jowls. "I didn't even see you when I grabbed that knife; skunk I had my mind on was back of the bar."

"The guy I slugged with the bottle?"

"No." He shook his head at my disbelief. "Pat's square enough. Grant's Pass was the bugger I was fixing to skewer. He come out of that door. While you was tangled with the barkeep, and before I could get a clean swing, he got back through it — you were right on his heels."

I couldn't help being astonished. I hadn't even suspicioned there'd been anyone ahead of me. "But that black haired — *Verdugo!* I'd of swore she was scairt half out of her wits."

"Sure. I guess she was. She's in love with the bugger, or thinks she is. My fault, in a way." He heaved a dour sigh. "I'd better tell you, I reckon. Kitty Verdugo's had some pretty hard knocks. She was born in Durango. When she was ten her pa and her mama were rubbed out by Apaches. I had her with the Sisters up to three-four months ago; told me I'd better let her come on home."

He studied a spell. "She works in this place; insists on earning her keep, and she does. But she's straight." His look challenged me.

"If that's so," I said, "and, like you claim, she's in love with this feller, why was you fixin' to heave that knife at him?"

"Damn two-bit romeo!" the fat man growled. "I ought to skin him alive, and mebbe I will if he don't stay clear of here! Just because she's a Mex. Jim, anyway, was a real gent once, but that damn Grant's Pass, as they've all took to calling him — Hell! Let's find something better than a woman-chasing pissant to occupy our jaws with. What'd you do to get that pair so put out with you?"

It was my turn to stumble around. Watching me, Dayne said, "Probably none of my business, but that Geet seems to have took a real violent dislike to you."

"Yeah." I couldn't honestly see what harm there was telling him. "He was botherin' that Drover's frail. I busted a chair over his mug. In front of witnesses."

"Sure enough? My!" he said, looking me over with a plainer interest. "Wonder you ain't got a lily in each fist." Rubbing his chins he considered me some more. "What's Longly's beef?"

I dug up a parched grin. Told him about that whippoorwill making off with my horse, about dragging my shooter and the marshal taking hold of me. "Never seein' that badge, I hung one on his kisser; I did help him up, though, even brushed him off," I said.

"And both of them plumb public," Jeff Dayne chuckled, shaking his head. "You really been humping, boy. Short of pulling our he-kangaroo's goatee you couldn't hardly have piled up more giref quicker." He peered a little more close at me. "You didn't by any chance tangle with Harra?"

"No," I said, and, tightening up, sloshed a look around the room. "There was somethin', though." I told how the marshal had happened to glom onto me, that set-to in the alley when Heidi had come busting out of that door trying to get loose of them unwanted attentions.

"This jigger," Dayne gruffed. "You happen to catch a look at —"

"Dang right I did. An' give him somethin' to remember me by! It was that chisel-faced jumper that went off on my horse!"

"Think you'd know him again?"

"He'll be packin' the mark of my gun barrel a spell." I told how I'd whacked him across the throat. "Even without that green an' black shirt —"

"Grant's Pass!" Dayne swore, quivering cheeks turning dark. "A pity you didn't break his damn neck!"

66

It was my turn to stare.

Account of Kitty Verdugo, of course, he had his mind on the man; but it did seem odd him naming him like that, and my description getting no response from the marshal. It seemed uncommon strange, particular remembering me telling Jim Longly the guy was out in that alley and him refusing even to look. I said so.

Jeff Dayne, settling back, continued to regard me. Out of the piled-up silence he finally said, "It's no great wonder. That maverick's his brother."

Hallelujah! I thought, and a whole heap of things suddenly begun to make sense.

The fat man grinned, but it was more like a grimace. His stare never left me. "You sure, boy, you ain't been sucked in by Mark Harra?"

I could feel the heat pounding into my cheeks. His look softened a little. "Sho," he said. "There's some things, at your age, can seem mighty personal. I reckon nobody likes to be taken for a fool."

I said, bitter, scowling, "Ain't been proved yet I have." My cheeks got hotter, remembering Jim Longly. "All right," I growled, "he offered me a job."

"Riding shotgun," Jeff Dayne nodded. "That figures, boy. You took it?"

"Suppose I did?"

"Then you're in for trouble. *Killin'* trouble."

VII

"Maybe you better chew that finer."

"Well," he pawed his perspiring chins some more. "He probably told you this camp's been kind of hard put during the past couple months to fetch in enough cash to meet payrolls, that certain unnamed parties have been grabbing all shipments. That about the gist of it?"

"Close enough."

Dayne nodded. "Then likely he pointed out about the only chance he can see to beat 'em is to get somebody the mask-and-gun gentry wouldn't have no reason to tie in with folks here, with the owners, that is. Some stranger, like yourself. Might be, trying to put the best face he could on it, he left it to you to come up with the way and means for delivery. I expect he offered a pretty good inducement. Like a hundred bucks, say, each trip regardless . . . and double that, mebbe, whenever you got it through?"

Talk about pulling hats out of a rabbit! "You was there?"

Dayne's round cheeks smiled. "Seemed a logical premise; but you mustn't overlook the trees for the woods. It will occur to you presently most of the practical steps have been taken."

I peered at him. "You tryin' to say I can't pull this off?"

Jeff spread his hands in a Mexican shrug. "You're missing the big thing."

"That there's a leak, you mean? But Harra claims — You think *he's* in back of it?"

"Heidi Quail's the camp's best authority there." He considered me patiently. "Best brains we've got have been chipping away at this but, like you, the most of them have rammed right over the unvarnished obvious."

"That feller! The guy they found in my room, was *he* diggin' into this?"

"Might have been," Jeff said without divulging an opinion. "Something else for you to take up with Heidi Quail."

"Why her?"

" 'You Bet' Farley, frock coat and all, was the nearest thing her daddy ever had to a law man. He was a disbarred attorney who made bottle money out of cards." Now

70

Dayne said, coming out with it, "You ought to line your sights more nearly at Tucson."

I could only stare, not making no sense of it. I had the feeling he thought I must be almighty stupid. But he just grinned, eyes still watching me. "You don't get it?"

I shook my head.

"Tucson," he said, "is where this whole thing takes off from. That's where the money is. No matter what schemes is hatched up here, that's where it's got to come from."

And Farley, I remembered, had been on a horse.

The night, I noticed, had cooled off considerable, or maybe it was me. There was still hitched horses at some of the racks, and almost out of sight, heavy loaded by the sound. Two freight outfits strung out for Galeyville was having hard pulling getting up the grade.

The street itself, here in town, loomed empty. Must be getting on toward morning, I thought, uncertainly considering the silent walks and peering, nervous, at the blacker slots between buildings. I'd refused Dayne's offer of a cot to tide me over. All the signs I'd been given a look at seemed to be arrowed in the direction of the Drover's as

71

the most likely place a man could get a tooth hold this side of the county seat.

It was there I had made the acquaintance of Geet. Outside the Drover's I'd run into the marshal and his horse-grabbing brother, Grant's Pass, who, by Jeff Dayne's tell, had been shining up to Kitty Verdugo, notwithstanding the back-alley didos he'd tried on Heidi Quail.

There was the girl herself, and me tied into it account of a guy who'd been teamed with her father being found dead inside the locked room she'd linked to me. And there was Jeff Dayne's testimonial naming her the camp's top authority on Harra.

All I'd got out of that place was trouble, yet here I was traipsing back again. I guess you'll think I had a hole in my head, but sense had nothing to do with it. The Drover's was where I had run into Harra, though I sure didn't look to find him there now.

Something about it — I wouldn't let myself believe it had anything to do with Heidi Quail; yet there was this pull, and her face was plainer to my mind right then than the handle of the shooter heavy banging against my hip.

I was drawn even while the thinking part of me, protesting, peered askance. And the nearer I come to that dim lobby lamp glow, away from what sound was left in the night, the more I had consciously to lift each boot. A danger-laced wildness seemed to lurk in the crouch of them bastardly shadows. I had to clamp my teeth — even then I was shaking. The ching of my spurs was like chimes in this stillness.

At the porch edge I twisted for a last cringing look. Nothing moved. I had an impulse to shout some crazy defiance if only to slap back the creep of that quiet.

I died a dozen deaths in the skreak of them planks. I went through the screen like a panicked badger.

The lobby was empty, the lamp turned low. It took pretty near forever to get up them stairs, what with squawks from my weight and the breath-caught stops while I hung there expecting half the camp to bust in.

I hung some more at the top, shaking, listening, eyes clapped to the number chalked on the door. The corridor's dimness was filled with the snores of sleeping men, and their smells crowded round till I could scarcely breathe. I got one fist around the door's china knob; finally got hold of enough wind to turn it. I careful pushed and it opened, so easy and unexpected I was halfway into the room before it come over me some barefoot walker was right on my heels.

I mighty near climbed the goddamn walls when a hand, steadily pushing, come against my back. "Step right on in." Just a whisper, it was, but fierce and ungiving as the prod of cold iron.

I wasn't in no good shape to argue. The door latch clicked and in that mealy black for about a split second I figured this whip-poorwill had shut me in. Then a match sprung to flame and in that orange light I saw Heidi Quail with her eyes like half dollars. They looked just as hard as the gun in her fist.

She said, blunt as always, "What do you think you're doing in here?"

"Well," I felt some put upon myself, "I sure didn't come to lovey-dovey with you!"

Her eyes, spilling out the kind of look a skunk might have got at a parlor social, took me in from head to foot. "Get the chimney off that lamp on the bureau." She bumped the wick with what was left of her match just before it got too short to hold.

I shoved the chimney back in its brackets. There was a pile of things I might have said, but I was still too riled from the fright she had give me to be digging up much in the way of chin music. She was barefoot, all right, had a blue wrapper round her, that red hair fanned out back of her shoulders. I reckoned she would just as like shoot as not.

"You can tell me," she said, "or you can talk to Jim Longly."

I sure wasn't minded to *habla* with him. "I don't expect you'll believe it," I finally got out, "but I come for another look at that stiff."

"You think I was fixing to keep him all night?"

I let that roll off. Then she said, more civil, "He was hit on the head, with a gun barrel probably. You keep sniffing around you could catch the same thing." Her eyes got all funny. "Why don't you get the hell out of here, Farris?"

I still ain't rightly figured how it happened — no such tomfoolery ever entered my head — but sudden-like both my arms was round her and both her arms was wrapped around me.

When we come up for air, first thing she said was, "Did you really come back for a look at Farley?"

"Sure," I said, and saw her eyes kind of darken. You'll reckon there's a heap I don't know about women. It's the golrammed truth — I don't make no bones of it. "But mostly," I said, "I come back to find out what you can tell me about Harra."

She seemed to be trying to read past them fool words, to guess what was behind them, to find the real me. I didn't catch that much then, it sort of come to me since. I saw her nose crinkle up, she give a bark of a laugh. Pulling loose, not making no sense, she said queerly, "I used to dream about this, thinking how it would be," and shook her head, mouth twisting. "I think you must have a one-track mind."

"Is he on the level?"

She considered me gravely. "I don't honestly know. The whole thing's so muddled — all those toughs he's hired, that crazy talk."

"But what do *you* think?"

"I think he's a crook! And a hypocrite, too! It was my pa, Farris, who made the discovery strike in these hills. There was nothing here then. What you see — all this," she flung out an arm, "came after. Post Oak, everything. There was a regular stampede; people came from all over. A lot of riffraff moved in — dice men, cardsharks, pimps and their women. You never saw such a mess. Inside six months there were twenty-three saloons!"

"All I've seen's three, and that's countin' Dayne's honky-tonk."

76

She nodded. "One by one Jeff took them over. Those he couldn't buy got busted up — mostly tent houses."

I said, scowling, "An' Harra?"

"Harra came later. Gave out to be interested in growing businesses, something, he said, that might give him a proper run for his money. He was thicker than splatter with Dayne for a spell, then they must have fell out. He got a horse and took to riding the hills. Then he hired him a crew, brought in some cows, bought a couple small ranches and threw them together. One he bought out was Jim Longly."

"And then put a star on him?"

"Jim was marshal already. Most people liked him. He was square, a good sport." She seemed lost in her thoughts.

"Humph!" I said. "What about this Grant's Pass?"

"After the ranch was sold he started running with Harra's bunch. Charley always was weak — he never used to be vicious. Getting free of his brother kind of went to his head. Took to calling himself that ridiculous name. He's been mixed up, I guess, in some pretty shady deals. He hires out his gun," she said, sounding worried.

"About your pa. If he made the original strike —"

"Never developed anything. His fun was in the hunting. He had this string of claims he'd staked but about all he did was gopher around. He turned up one good pocket; it went into this hotel. About the time Dayne and Harra got fed up with each other Harra made Pa an offer for those Aravaipa claims; I don't think Pa had any notion of selling. He never talked that way. Then, last May, that's a year ago, he went off with a burro, hankering to turn up fresh ground."

Her look turned grim. "The afternoon of the day Pa set off, Mark Harra told around he had bought those claims."

I said, "Mebbe he did," but not too hopeful. Some things she hadn't put to words I could feel. The dark thoughts looking out of her, the lift of her chin, churned uncomfortably through me. "What did your dad say?"

"They never gave him the chance. He was found the next week at the bottom of a shaft."

We stared at each other. "What's the duff on this Farley?"

"He was supposed to have looked over the papers for Pa. That's what they said, anyway."

"An' he give 'em the nod?"

"Apparently."

"If he hadn't been killed — What happened to the money?"

"It's a pretty good question not to ask around here. Harra says he paid cash." She smiled wryly. "Thirty thousand."

Pretty raw, I thought, whistling. "Farley never said nothing?"

"He suggested I take a trip to the patent office. Everything had been transferred; there was nothing I could do. For a 'dollar and other valuable considerations' Harra had a clear title. The property is recorded as The Twelve Apostles Mine. I could have howled, but who would notice? Those gunfighters are a pretty good insurance." She said with them gold-brown eyes digging into me, "How do you feel about working for him now?"

I felt sick, no use denying it. I told her what Dayne had said about that deal. She said, "I wish you hadn't —" Her eyes got big. *"Killing trouble."* It was pretty near a whisper. She got hold of my arm, kind of hugging it to her. "Oh, Clint!" she said in what was almost a wail. "Don't do it!"

79

VIII

I was fed to the gills.

All the sneers and harassments, them contrived indignities, the whole sorry mishmash of what I amounted to, rose up like a maddening flood in rebellion against the lousy run of cards life had chucked me. I said, never thinking how it might look to her, "It could be the last chance I ever have to do anything!"

"But he's *right,* Clint — Jeff's right! They've killed every man who's been put on that run. Don't you *see?* They can't afford to let anyone live who might name them!"

Every snarling misery boxed into my memory broke loose in wild yammer to temper and toughen this brash determination, to set it up like veins in stone, her resistance curing it as smoke cures meat. I had the bit in my teeth and no power could turn me.

She had sense enough to know when she was whipped. A forlorn kind of sigh came out of her, the barest tremble of sound, but no tears, no reproaches.

I saw her then, the shaken look of her cheeks and them staring eyes. "It's the only way we can ever know the brass tacks truth of who's pullin' the strings — whether Harra's the one or it's somebody else."

"When will you go?"

I patted her shoulder. "I'll go see Harra now."

"Oh, Clint, *do* be careful!"

"I'll be careful," I said, seeing a number of things I hadn't noticed before. The dark ins and outs of this thing had no end to them, wheels within wheels, but behind all the greed, all these bits of skulduggery, there'd be one biggest spider that had to be stepped on — one weaver, one planner all the rest was tied into.

"What can I do that will help?" she said then.

I looked at my thoughts. "You reckon Dayne's back of these stickups?"

She stood there a moment. "Jeff can be pretty ruthless; I don't think he's dishonest."

"Do you know how Farley got into this room, or where Geet got that key?"

She shook her head. "I didn't know Farley had got back; he's been away. As for the key, anybody, I guess, could have slipped in and got it. I picked it up after you'd gone and put it back on the rack."

"Dayne," I said, "seems to figure if there's a leak it's at the Tucson end. All the arrangements, he thinks, has to be fixed there. On account of the money."

Something jumped in her look. "Farley! Do you suppose that's where he's been? Perhaps," she said, brightening, "you ought —"

"No! You put your finger on it. The nub of this thing is in the grabbin' itself, the fact they can't afford to let a witness get away. I don't know how it is, or why, but —"

"Farley was never a witness, Clint."

"He was *supposed* to have witnessed the sale of them claims. And he goes off on this trip. Maybe his conscience caught up with him, or mebbe," I said, "he got nosey. He certainly got rubbed out, that's for sure!" I took a turn of the room, wheeled abruptly and faced her. "What was you doin' back there with that horse thief?"

She half opened her mouth, then her chin come up, closing it. With her eyes gone tight and hard she lammed past, slipping down them stairs like a wet-footed cat.

I could have kicked myself when I seen how it sounded; the fact that I'd spoke like she was something I owned wasn't figured to calm her ruffled feelings much neither. I reckoned I had better stay out from under foot until that redheaded temper got worked off a little.

Digging out my watch I found with surprise it was a sight nearer daylight than I'd any idea of. Another hour at most was all I had if I was minded to be out of Post Oak by sun-up; and, besides seeing Harra, I still had a horse to find.

It didn't seem too likely I'd be getting one from Harra. There was that livery Heidi had mentioned, but them eight paper dollars I had wouldn't buy much more than a wore-out bridle, not in a camp like this anyway. I thought of Jeff Dayne.

But that wasn't quite the same. The loan of a branded horse, any pony that could be traced back, could tie him to me a heap closer than he might care for. Still thinking about him I blew out the light.

He'd already took up for me.

Leaving the door where it was I stepped over to the window which was in the back wall, and, summoning what tatters of patience I could, got up the sash, trying hard to keep it quiet. A mutter of voice sound come up from somewhere. Mighty careful, I peeked out.

Like I'd half suspicioned there was a piece of roof, about a four-foot ledge, directly below. This shrunk my view of what else might be down there, like maybe Jim Longly or that gun-throwing brother who had got me warned not to be here come morning. This piece of roof could be ten foot from the grond. There was an empty pen sticking out of the dark and a couple of scraggly hackberries beside it, but too far out to hold any help. By hanging from my fingers, if I could land and stay on it, that ledge shouldn't be more than a three foot drop.

I pushed a leg over the sill and, without waiting longer, skinned over and hung. I had some pretty bleak thoughts before I finally let go. The damned ledge pitched some worse than I'd figured and there was nothing to grab onto. That slant threw me out. I lost my balance and went over.

I banged into the ground like a broken roped bucket hitting the bottom of a well. Felt like every bone in me was busted, and half of them driven clean on through to China.

No telling how long I lay there. It was hard to get back even enough wind to cuss with. To tell you frank, I might of been there till Christmas, I was that scairt to move, if the hard slap of boots hadn't jerked me out of it. They had come off wood and was thumping round the Drover's like the devil beating tanbark. I had one thought — a lamp bright picture of cold-jawed Jim Longly — and come up off that ground like a cottontail rabbit.

I got clear; don't ask me how I done it. My hide ached like mules had been drove over me. Every bone let out a shouting, every muscle stiff as a Charley horse, but I run. I guess nobody ever seen nothing like it. I sure as hell wasn't seeing much either till I come hard against the Boll Weevil's back door, and nothing I tried would by God get it open!

Of course I didn't pound; I wasn't trying to hang up no record for racket. All I wanted was to climb on a horse and get me out of this camp ahead of Longly; I had a mighty bleak hunch if he put hands on me again, any hereafter I had coming wouldn't last no longer than two bits in a poker game.

When the roaring inside me began to slack off some I seen pretty clear what a fool play I'd made, not in ducking that marshal but scratching at this door. There wouldn't be no horse inside a dang honky-tonk!

Time was getting away from me. The shadows was beginning to show streaks of gray and I could hear empty wagons rattling up through the shale on their way to the mines. I could strike out for Tucson without seeing Harra, but getting that money was going to need his okay.

Then I noticed this shed off the alley back of Dayne's. It had closed Dutch doors like they put on horse palaces and, just on the chance there might be a nag in there, I cut over for a look.

There was a length of strap iron across both doors and a hasp, but somebody had been in too much of a hurry. The padlock holding this rig hadn't latched — a piece of sheer luck if I had ever bumped into one.

Before lifting it free I sloshed a glance at the roundabout shadows. The animal inside begun to show his impatience. A good sign, I thought, because no coldblooded cart horse would paw the ground that way.

A cooler hand, maybe, might of read that sign different; I might have myself if I'd been under less pressure. I got the strap off, all thumbs though I was, and swung open both doors.

It was still pretty dark. About all I could be sure of was this big, muscled rump and a sleek combed-out tail ending short of clean hocks. A dark bay or black, and he was snorting now, nervous. There was the shine of his eyes peering over a shoulder. Tied, he was, too.

I was watching them legs, edging in to get round him, when a girl's angry voice cried, "What are you up to!"

Holding a bucket, she wasn't three steps away. Kitty Verdugo, and all set to yell.

Great! I thought, disgusted. A caught horse thief! No better than Grant's Pass, and without —

She come forward, peering sharper. "Oh! It's you; Mother of God but you gave me a turn! I thought . . . did Jeff send you out here to take care of Águila?"

Right on a platter. You couldn't have it no better, and all I done was just stand there, goggling, them words of hers squeezing my insides until it hurt.

"No," I said, like a gold-plated ninny. "I was fixin' to grab that bronc an' take off!"

IX

You'll think I should have been bored for the simples.

I was aghast at myself. Against the brightening outside light I could see the comb poking up from her head. No need of them eyes or the shock of her mouth with her shape gone so still in the gray of that doorhole.

Then she laughed. I felt like Jericho's walls about the time old Gabe bent to pick up his tooter. "When you're finished," she said, "you'd better come in to breakfast."

I stared after her, bug-eyed.

Sick with myself I picked up the measure of oats she'd come in with.

No telling, when I didn't come round, what she'd say to Jeff Dayne, or what he would do when this stud turned up missing. The horse was plain enough now for me to know he cost money. He was short on the top with a long underline that held out the promise of both speed and bottom. I dumped the oats in his feed trough and, while he was eating, found his rig and got him ready. I wasn't hunting no hay. Quick as he quit chewing I shoved a bit in his month, rammed the bridle over his ears and, hanging onto the cheek strap, danced him through them open Dutch doors.

Hauled up, peering, I could scarcely believe it. Fog, like gray smoke, was thick outside as feathers in a pillow. No sign of the Boll Weevil — ten foot off I could only just barely see the end of its dock.

The horse mighty near got away while I was staring. I piled onto him then, not taking no chances. Moving him past where I figured Dayne's place was it come over me sudden I hadn't any notion where I was supposed to find Harra. Looked like he'd of told me. If he had I couldn't recollect.

I got onto the street, still fretting and fuming, knowing the guy would have a office here someplace, anyways a house — a gent important as he was.

It seemed lighter out here, the fog not so clinging but what you could pick out the nearer buildings with the tatters of mist piled up in layers around the shine of whatever lamps was yet showing. But you couldn't read signs without getting right up to them. The only live things in sight, and that wasn't fooling me, was a couple hitched broncs humped over a tie rack.

Someone had told me the name of Harra's mine was The Twelve Apostles, not that I was fixing to stomp around hunting it. I wasn't craving at all to run into Jim Longly or them *buscadero* bully-puss Johns he chummed round with. Nor it didn't look smart to duck into the Boll Weevil, though that was what I done. I was too durn scairt of picking up a blue whistler to stay any longer on that street than I had to.

Knotting Águila's reins round a porch post I pushed through Dayne's slatted half-leafs, heart pounding, knowing right then I wasn't cut out for this.

The only guy in there was a bent-over swamper spreading sawdust from a bucket who didn't even bother to twist his neck or look up.

"Where'll I find Mark Harra?"

"Sleeps over his office."

"Where would that be?"

He sloshed a look at the clock. " 'Leven doors down, other side of the street." Dumping the last of his sawdust he reached for a gaboon.

I backed out, slipped the reins and got into the saddle.

Eleven doors down. Seemed a powerful piece, looking off through the curl of that fog. It was thinner, maybe lifting, with a ground breeze rolling up from them south flats. Trying back lots would be risky, too. I nudged the stud with a knee.

He moved away from Dayne's porch, and I could tell straightaway he was feeling them oats. It took a strong hand to keep him down to a head-shaking three-cornered walk.

Part way down a guy stepped out, ducked under a hitch-rail and come up, staring. My heart come up, too. It started beating my windpipe. Just as I come even, trying to make up my mind if I should reach or sink steel, the galoot turned away and staggered off between buildings. Which didn't leave much chance for studying doorholes or shadows.

It was while, soaked with sweat, I was trying to get back some of the breath I had lost, I saw the place I was hunting. No lights showing. Evidently he hadn't got up yet.

I scowled, peering round. I sure didn't want to leave this horse on the street. Something then, some skitterish notion, hauled my eyes to the place next beyond.

Every hair come off my scalp stiff as wire. It was the Drover's and Geet, in the lamplit lobby gone as still as a Injun, was staring straight at me!

It was kind of a shock.

I must have hung froze a dozen seconds hand-running before, with a shuddery grab at fresh breath, it passed through my head he hadn't seen nothing, not with the shine of that lamp in his face.

Not exactly calm, but certainly trying to be reasonable careful, I put Dayne's stud up the crack of dark passage between Harra's building and the shuttered store this side.

Getting off that street seemed a likely thing to do. Smartest move I could make with this big devil under me was to get as far and fast as I might. There was too many here who would like nothing better than to stretch my hide to the nearest wall, and Jeff, soon's he went for this horse, would be one of them. You just can't argue with a stem-winding bullet!

But it was in my mind, too, I hadn't come no great ways in my campaign to start over. I'd never had it so rough. And, besides, there was Heidi. Seemed the least I could do was give Harra's proposition the whirl I'd already promised.

Behind his place I was anchoring Águila in a half bare stand of yellowing salt cedar when this bang hit my ears like a burst paper sack. First thing I thought of was a coat-muffled shooter. Geet jumped into my head, and I come within a ace of getting back on that horse.

I even had a foot up.

It was uncommon hard not to follow it into leather, but someway I couldn't. Easing it down, watchful as spiders, I catfooted closer to the back side of Harra's, drawn there like a rope was hauling me.

Though a full two storeys, tall enough for his importance, it wasn't much better than a square mud box, not near so deep nor broad as The Drover's. Didn't look to have more than a room to each level. Like a blockhouse, kind of, or the tower to something that had been tore down. There was a door in the end and one lone window with a pulled-flat shade that, even as I watched, turned lemon bright, throwing out the black shapes of two bent-over men.

With the flare of that lamp, and them shadows to scrinch at, I guessed the sound I had heard was a door, maybe snatched by the wind from a careless hand; might even of been the one they slipped in by. What really shook me was the astonishing resemblance of this nearest bent shape to the ga-loot who had told me to be out of here by morning. My cold-jawed friend, the Post Oak badge-toter.

If this was him, and I'd have bet on it, who was with him? And what were they doing in Harra's office?

The other shape was too dim and muzzy for any clear shot at a name to clap on it. You couldn't begin to even gage the size of him but it was plain enough he was teamed with Jim Longly. Geet, more than like, or his Grant's Pass brother!

The window was shut. All I could catch was a grumble of voices, no words, nothing usable. Even a ear against the wall didn't help. I couldn't think waiting was going to get me much, either. No matter which hole I covered there was no guarantee they wouldn't leave by the other. And, scrooched up against the place that way, I kept thinking what a bind I'd be in if someone else come along or that big stud of Dayne's nickered.

Then, impatient, he suddenly did.

Both shadow shapes stiffened. I had just about time to go into my rabbit act. Fright and despair, those insufferable well-wishers, was shoving me hard toward a lunge for the tules. Sick with the bitterness of self-disgust I watched for the lamp in Harra's office to die.

Before they could kill it I was at the door, hammering like mad in the brashness of panic.

X

"What the hell!" Harra snapped, angrily yanking it open after freeing the bar.

Light come against my face like a mallet, and over his shoulder the marshal's elk stare was as coldly ungiving as a wall of dressed granite.

"Well, if it ain't the kid from Bitter Crick!" With a jeering laugh he stepped away from the desk. Then the grin quit his face. "You playin' stickup or somethin'?"

With that gun in my fist I felt a sure enough fool. There was nobody else, just them. And though his chin hair bristled there was nothing about Harra's scowling attention to suggest I'd come onto things he didn't want told.

But there was something, the feel you get around a spooky bronc, a restless kind of chilled steel waiting that kept me hung to that shooter.

The glint in Longly's stare got brighter,

and again I saw on the screen of my mind this pair with their heads bent over that desk. What were they up to? *Why were they here at such an hour with the shades drawn?*

This fix was bulging worse with each breath. Even with this hog-leg affronting the proprieties I wasn't going to keep them stood up much longer without I was ready to shoot or be shot at.

"How's the trumpet of the Lord this mornin'?" I said, watching Jim Longly settling into his tracks. He had a shorter fuse than what was built into Harra. His patience was thinner, or maybe his conscience had a trickier load.

He looked just about up to letting go all holds when Harra, coolly nodding, took the play away from him. "I suppose you're here, Farris, about that — Oh, you needn't mind Jim; he's as much concerned as —" He broke off to say testily, "You can put up that pistol!" and to peer at me sharper round the beak of his nose. "It seems I won't be needing your good efficiency."

"Mean you've hired someone else!"

A polite regret looked out of his smile.

"Him?" I said with a flick of my gun snout.

"Point is, you weren't around when I needed you. Many are called but few are chosen," he said, warming up to it and getting right into his hell-fighting voice. "When the bridegroom cometh —"

I said, "Never mind that," beginning to think I'd got hold of something. "If no one's been gettin' any payrolls through — *Stand still, Marshal!*"

Them two swapped glances. Longly's shifted weight brought his burnt-leather look a little deeper into shadow and I said, pushing the thought around, "A pretty slick stunt, sending Farley up with it, then shutting his mouth."

Harra's face jerked around. He seemed to catch himself, chuckling, but it didn't quite hide the wicked shine of his eyes.

"Looks like I better find a place for you, Farris."

"I don't want no place like you found for that shyster!"

"Well," Harra said, and turned unwinkingly moveless while the marshal's look got tighter and darker and, too late, I saw where this brashness had took me.

Only a fool could doubt any longer what was going on here, or what was back of it; and Longly it looked like, account of his brother, had been sucked into where he had to go along.

The door I'd come in by was back of me someplace, but if he went for his shooter I was due to get planted. Placed like they was with six feet between them it wasn't in the cards I'd be able to get both.

Harra, grinning, didn't bother to speak.

A Mexican standoff. Sweat was cold on my skin. I felt the pressure of panic.

Like there was sand in his voice, Jim Longly said, "You don't want to be no dead hero, do you?"

Desperate to get him stopped I cried, "I won't go alone."

"Take Jim," Harra laughed, stepping back.

I saw Longly's cheeks, wild as a willie's. The contempt and easy coldblooded scorn in which Harra without hesitation had withdrawn his support, clearly had pushed the man beyond reach of anything.

His mouth went back like a cornered rat's. Like enough my own probably done the same. First shot, I was thinking, better go for the lamp or Harra would have me before I could swing. *And it would have to be blind!* I didn't dare twist my look off the marshal.

I was tipping it up, praying for luck, when across the room the front door banged open. One frightened glimpse I caught of her eyes before all hell jumped out of the skillet. The lamp went up in a burst of blue flame. Slugs, whistling and whining, smacked into the walls as, driven from a crouch, I went through the window in a frantic dive.

A tin roof wouldn't have made more racket. Shots, shouts and cursing built a bedlam behind as I come off the ground in a rolling lunge, shook loose of the shade and pelted for the cedars where I'd left Dayne's horse.

He was there, snorting and pawing in a lather of excitement; my breath was like a saw ripping logs as I fumbled, all thumbs, to get the damned knot out of them tangled reins. I could hear Harra shouting, and the snarls of the marshal above the scared scrabble of the girl's frightened questions.

My time was shorter than the tail holt on a bear. Even as the reins come free and I went up, blue whistlers begun to slam through the cedars. I raked Águila both sides with the steel and we tore out of that brush with the guns popping back of us and lead swarming thick as a hatful of hornets.

Cuffing him around I got him lined out on a uphill scramble pointed toward the Globe road. It climbed north through the mountains but, quick as I figured we'd cut off Harra's view, I cut him sharp right, going down a long tangent in a slather of shale that fetched us, shaking, into the top end of town. Not waiting to catch no breath but walking him careful through that gray chintzy light, I come up back of The Drover's.

Crazy? You bet! Yet who but a fool would think to look for me there? Not them, I didn't reckon; and seemed like I was right. It was quiet next door, as a goosehair pillow. Looked like they had all took off hellity-larrup.

I come out of the saddle, softly tapped her back door, hanging onto the reins and peering two ways to once. Don't think I wasn't nervous; I felt about as unlikely as a tender-foot trapper slicing out his first skunk. I only hoped she'd had time to get over her mad, and that wasn't all I was thinking of, either. There was still more than somewhat about this Post Oak mess I hadn't caught up with. I didn't understand even all I knew about it.

When no one answered I tried to ease the door open. Like I figured, it was barred.

I could feel the sweat cracking through my hide and a bunch of cold prickles chasing up and down the back of my neck. I was scared to call out, afraid to leave without seeing her.

Being timid's plain hell. I must of died a dozen deaths scrinched up against that door hanging onto my breath, picturing a hundred things that could happen and wondering, back of everything else, if Geet was still hunkered alongside that desk.

I rapped again, about ready to fly when sound come barefootin' up to the door.

"Who's there?" Heidi called, no louder than a cricket.

"Me," I said. "You gonna stand there and yak?"

Looked like, for a minute, she didn't figure to talk no way. "Is Geet in there?" I said, some urgent.

The bar snicked back. She pulled the door open and, hand on it, stood there, me feeling about as welcome as a mut coming home with a nasty bone.

Her eyes come wide open. She had seen the gun. "Well!" she sniffed, "so you *were* mixed up —" It was then, I guess, that she took in the horse.

"You gone plumb loco?"

"Shh . . ." I growled. "Not so golrammed loud! All I want —"

"Git in here!" Her arm shot out, fastened into my shirtfront. You wouldn't think, for her size, she had that much strength. But the next thing I knew, there I was in the kitchen, still gripping them reins, with the door shut behind me.

XI

I held the reins out, waggling them, looking, I reckon, more stupid than usual.

No one had run off with Heidi's tongue. "You think I'm going to take *him* in, too? Throw them down," she cried, "he ain't goin' no place!"

The kind of look she give me — without it come from his wife — no guy with gumption would of took for a minute. She stepped back, arms akimbo. "What have you been up to?"

"Geet?" I said, nervous, peering over her shoulder.

"He went hightailin' out of here soon's that row started. Come on, let's have it, who've you killed now?"

So I unlimbered my tale. She stood taking it in, saying never a word till I come to where Kitty Verdugo showed up. "Whatever that bunch has been up to," I said, "she's into it plumb to them black Spanish eyes!"

"She's straight," Heidi said. "She probably stepped over there hunting for Charley."

"Charley . . . who's he?"

"The marshal's brother. Grant's Pass."

"Oh," I said, scowling, reminded of the horse I'd been done out of. "Mebbe."

"What are you trying to do now? They'll be back, you know."

"That's why I come over here." I put up my shooter, annoyed that she figured I couldn't see that. "Seems like Harra's been havin' a pretty good thing, sendin' guys down there secret, then rubbin' 'em out after they've fetched up his payrolls."

"You're just guessing," she said.

"I ain't got no proof but . . . I thought you was bustin' to fix his clock!"

"What's the point in all this? He's not paying his miners."

"Prob'ly usin' it," I growled, "to pay off that gun crew that's pullin' the stickups. Cripes! He can afford to close shop if the rest of these owners can't take out no ore. An' if they can't pay their men —"

"What I told you straight off. If the others get hard up enough he can buy them out at ten cents on the dollar. Maybe if you talked to them —"

"You think they'd listen? Hell," I said,

"you was right in the first place. Proof's what we need, and I've a notion. . . . But I've got to have help."

"I'll help."

I told her, scowling, "You're a prejudiced party. I've got to have someone these owners'll listen to. This Harra's dug in, but if he's sent for more cash —"

"He won't stop his *own* man. He don't have to; you've shown that. If you've got it in mind to catch them red-handed we better put out some bait." When I stared, she said: "A payroll shipment for one of the other mines. By stage, of course, but *secret.*"

"How you gonna work that? An' if it's secret," I said.

"They'll get onto it," she told me. "How secret did *you* stay?" She caught up her hat. "I better get moving. That feller Harra hired in your place, has he gone yet?"

"You seem to be wearin' the pants for this deal!"

She come back to put her hand on my arm. "If we pull this off it will be a joint effort, Clint. Farris, Quail and Company." She wrinkled her nose at me. Squeezing, she said, "I'll go see if old Phipstadt will risk a little cash."

"And who do you figure to talk into siding?"

"Jeff Dayne will go with you. They'll take *his* word."

It was him I'd had in mind. But now, with her putting his name in the pot, I couldn't see him for hell. I said, "How about Longly? He's the badge-packer here."

She looked her surprise. "I thought you reckoned he was tied in with Harra."

"How do you know that saloon keeper ain't? You forgettin' Verdugo? Come right in, she did, never a knock! Besides," I said, scowling, "what about his horse?"

She considered me, sighing. "Jeff told you about Kitty. Where else would she go to find out about Charley?" It was plain she thought I was being unreasonable. Probably I was, but a man likes to feel he's got *some* of the answers — once, anyway.

She said with that gamin grin on her mouth: "As for the horse, why don't you step over and see Dayne about him? A brash, string, upright, handsome galoot like you shouldn't mind facing up to a trifle of that sort." And off she went, with a sniff, trailing trickles of laughter.

I felt like the fool with the sack at a snipe hunt, hot as a blanket after a hard ride. She could sure cut a man down to size in short order.

I went out with the reins and climbed into the saddle. She hadn't left me much choice. What I ought to have done, thinking back to it now, was taken Águila and dug for the tules; or maybe this was just the spleen working out of me. I'd been dancing to other folks' tunes all my life. A hard turn to drop. But I had come to Post Oak to face up to myself, and if I was ever going to do it right now was the time.

"I'll show her!" I growled, and kneed the horse around, right into the street and down its dead center like a storybook sure-shot, ignoring the stares I could feel swinging after me. Straight up to the front of Dayne's honky-tonk I rode and, jaws clenched, stepped down.

Tossing the reins over the pole I went in, remembering that other time. "Boss here?"

The guy in the apron jerked a thumb toward the office.

"Go tell him," I said, "there's a horse thief out here wants to swap *habla* with him."

I don't know what I expected. Not what I got. Jeff Dayne's bulging cheeks and three chins showed up, with the apron's popped eyes goggling back of one shoulder. I couldn't read what he thought from that moon of a face, gage his intent or temper. I stood brittle stiff but I stood, damn her eyes!

Dayne suddenly chuckled. "Hi, kid," he grinned. "Better get that chip down offen your muscle an' tie into a drink before them knees of yours give out complete. Fetch it over to that corner table," he told the barkeep. Looking, I suspect, pretty hangdog and sheepish, I followed him over and took the chair he pushed out.

I perched on it like a caught fence-crawler. Reckon my tongue must of run off and hid. This shaped up to be harder even than I had figured. Sweat moved around on my lip like a fly and, sudden, I couldn't seem to hold it no longer. "You'll find the damn horse tied out front!" I blurted.

The apron come with a glass and a bottle, plunked them down and went back to the bar. "Go ahead," Dayne said. "I sell the stuff but I don't have to drink it."

I told him, glowering, I didn't have to either. And there we set with that table between us and the not-knowing silence piling up chunk on chunk till the durn squirming weight of it was not to be borne. "He ain't hurt," I snarled, "if that's what you're thinkin'!"

"I haven't lost any horse."

I looked at him, hard. Borrowed or whatever, I had still took that stud, and if he figured to overlook it I aimed to have him say so. "He come out of your shed."

"Must be Kitty's horse, Águila."

It took me square in the wind. *Was this what had fetched her over to Harra's?*

"If you were going to light out," Jeff Dayne said, "why didn't you?"

"I took the horse to go after that job. When I got to Harra's place the marshal was with him. Harra told me he'd already hired somebody." I mentioned how it had been, me sandwiched between them and Longly all set to go for his shooter, and the girl showing up and me knocking the lamp out. "You know this bunch a sight better than I do; you reckon he's fixin' to send Longly after it?"

The fat man, studying his fists, finally shrugged. "Hard to tell."

I put him next to our notions about Farley. All the change I got from that was a nod. A fish-belly shine was beginning to come out of him.

"If it's Águila," I growled; and his look, coming back from some far place, kind of tightened and shuddered. "Take the horse," he muttered. "I'll take care of Kitty."

Something about the way that sounded

pulled my eyes around. If what he meant was he'd 'square' it, why hadn't he said so?

"If you're trying to get rid of me —"

Starting to get up, he settled back with a growl. "Them boys, you know, ain't playin' for peanuts." He looked like he wished I'd drop into some hole.

What I couldn't figure quite was why. But it come over me now with considerable astonishment all that yap he had give me before about Tucson was a pile of damn hogwash, something connived to get me out of this camp. And I looked at him harder, trying to see how this fit.

"Keep away from them, kid, or you'll end up on a shutter."

And then a sigh rumbled out of him. "So she got to you, did she? I was afraid she would." He said, leaning forward, "Don't it scare you thinkin' of what happened to Farley?"

"There's other things scares me worse." I was able, even, to grin at him a little; and I saw his look darken. Some of the things that was bottled inside him, desperation and anguish, began to come through, but I was figuring now we spoke the same lingo.

I said, more confident, "Your hands've been tied account of Verdugo. You're too square a gent to rest easy on your butt while the rest of this camp gets took for a clean-in'."

The big feller snorted.

He took off his cheaters, puffing on them, rubbing them. The shape of his cheeks seemed more forlorn than angered. It was hard to be sure with a face smooth as his. I said, "We ain't got much time."

He hooked the wires back over his ears. "You just can't romp around exterminatin' people."

"If we come onto 'em while they was up to their necks in it."

"You wouldn't have nothing but punkin-seeds, Farris."

"If we caught Geet —" I began, but Jeff shook his head.

"Geet's just a bully boy, the threat, not the medicine. To implicate Harra you've got to hit closer. Bustin' the gang up ain't going to stop him."

"Grant's Pass Charley?"

Them cheaters hid the look of Jeff's eyes, but a plain reluctance was in every line of him. This was why he'd set back and stayed out of it, account of that crazy mixed-up girl that had it stuck in her head Longly's black sheep brother was some kind of tin-pants saint on horseback.

"Well, hell," I said, "she's gonna be hurt

111

no matter *what* you do. If she up an' runs off with him —"

Dayne sighed again. "Yep." He scrubbed a sleeve across his jaw. "Charley's the nub of it. He's the lodestone that's hung round her neck. Harra's blackjack."

I saw it, now. All the bits clicked together. Blood was thicker than water; Longly went along because there was nothing else he could do. Harra pulled the strings around here, and the rest of these yaps was more ready to cut off a hand or both legs than bring on a visit from the boss-man's adjuster.

"But, damnit —" I growled.

Jeff shook his head. "People, kid, once they've give in, will take a mighty lot to hang onto what they've got. Most of them's still living. The memory of them that's gone works for Harra — that's his system. Hope, luck, and some reminders of Charley."

He blew out a bitter sigh and got up. "Fork that horse, kid, and —"

"Help's what I'm huntin', not a way to get out of this!"

"You can't buck the whole camp."

"If we can catch them redhanded —"

"God, but you're stubborn! Look, you can't catch the ones that will do any good. Grant's Pass and Harra! How will you get at them?"

"Bait. Heidi's goin' to have Phipstadt —"

His narrowing stare had gone over my shoulder. I heard the batwings slap shut and steps coming lightly over the floor, and just behind me they stopped. Heidi said, "It's all fixed. The money'll come up tomorrow by stage out of Tucson. Every last nickel Phipstadt's got in the bank."

XII

Dayne, not much liking it, finally give in.

He didn't think they'd go for it. Even if they did we didn't know, he said, where Harra's hyenas would make their play. If we cleared these hurdles and managed to save Phipstadt's cash he still couldn't figure an outside chance of bagging Grant's Pass without killing the bugger. "We have to bring him in dead, what the hell have you accomplished!"

"At least," I said, "we'll have proved it can be done."

The fat man, snorting, went off with Heidi to sack up the grub.

It didn't look too promising even to me; but if someone back along had been willing to put his neck out maybe, I thought, there'd been no need of this now. You never knew what you could do till you tried.

And there was Heidi, of course, and that Twelve Apostles Mine her dad had been done out of, not to mention his death, which could be laid, it seemed now, at the door of the marshal's shoot-and-run brother along with a passel of other people's troubles. And, back of everything else, I still had to know if it was guts I was packing around or just fiddlestrings.

When Jeff showed up with the grub, and two filled canteens sloshing round on their straps, there was something different in the cut of his eye which impelled me, caught up, to peer hard at the girl. "What's the matter?"

"Nothing the matter with me." She tossed her head. "Jeff can't get used to the notion of havin' me along."

"You! Hell's fire, you're not goin'!"

"Who got Phipstadt to put up the money? Whose idea was it that we catch them redhanded? Who," she said, chin up, "has a better right?"

"But . . . but . . . for the love of Mike, Heidi! A deal like this — ain't no *place* for a girl! Godfries!" I said. "Them buggers ain't playin' for peanuts, you know! When them guns get to poppin' —"

"Mine will be poppin', too! Take the grub," she said, "and let's get to whackin'."

She took the canteens from Dayne and, slipping the straps bandoleer-fashion over

115

her shoulders, went off through the batwings without a backward look. Jeff, wryly grinning, handed me the grub sack, then got me a rifle and two boxes of cartridges. "Happy days," he said. "I'll catch up with you later."

We camped that evening in a tall stand of jackpines thirty miles south and not too far off the Tucson road. While I took care of the horses Heidi opened the grubsack and fixed us some sandwiches. I could of done with some java but she wouldn't risk a fire. We washed them down with some of the warm water from the canteens Jeff had loaned us.

We were still in hill country. After the sun sank behind the Tortolitas it began to cool off. I fetched Heidi her blankets and got into my brush jacket. We hadn't swapped much talk in the past three-four hours and now, with darkness settling over the land, a kind of constraint sprung up between us. She put her back to a tree, blanket over her shoulders, and I hunkered against another. Tongue-tied and grumpy I scowled at my thoughts, wondering if Harra's gunnies was still combing the ridges. They must have found out by now we had skipped. Once clear of town we'd got onto the Tucson wagon road and hadn't left enough tracks to trip up an ant.

We watched a yellow moon creep over Biscuit Peak and somewhere off in that lonesome quiet a coyote pack set up its awful yammer. "You warm enough?" I said, and saw her face tip toward me.

"I'm all right."

"Tomorrow," I said, "you better take the Winchester and let me have that .45-90."

Everything considered it was a hell of a conversation. For two people that was supposed to be gone on each other we was sure letting a pile of good time slip away. But there was things on my mind.

I don't know when I quit thinking. Next thing I knew, something had hold of my shoulder. I jerked open my eyes, some surprised to find it wasn't more than a cuss and two snorts to wide-awake morning.

In this cold gray-shadowed time that was not quite night nor yet day neither, the bent-over blob of the girl's concerned face swept the cobwebs out of me as nothing else could have.

"Clint," she whispered, "there's something out there!" and pressed her dad's rifle into my hands.

I don't know if it was the comforting weight of that gun or her fright — the dependence and trust — that done it but, strangely, I felt cool as a well chain. My ears caught the fox-like drift of his progress, the low scuff of sound coming over damp needles, the nerve-twisting pauses while he peered and listened.

I got out of my boots. "Stay put," I growled, and the confidence I felt was like a heady wine. I knew exactly what to do, just how to go about it, circling the sounds to come up downwind of him. *Regular Tom Horn!* I told myself, marveling.

Off thirty yards I picked up the dim shape of him, writhing like smoke between the poles of the pines.

I snicked back the bolt.

The horse threw up his head with a snort, froze beneath the clamped muscles of his rider. The guy, never twisting his head, said, "Farris?"

A quiver run through me. "Why the hell didn't you sing out!" And Jeff Dayne's laugh only riled me fiercer. It was good, just the same, to know he had got here. He was the chiefest thing I'd been wondering about.

Even Heidi looked pleased in the freshening light. "Coffee, Jeff?"

He peered around as we come up. "I expect we can risk it."

"Better keep it small," I grumbled.

While I got into my boots he give us the news, all, anyways, he figured was good for us. Harra, it seemed, was still around town but his crew was gone, presumably off to catch up work at the ranch. "Looks," Dayne grinned, "like they figure you've sloped; Longly's gone, too." He glanced around at Heidi. "Put in most of yesterday watching your place. Just short of chow he rode off, pointin' south."

Right at that moment I didn't care where he'd went. Suppose, I was thinking, we'd read Farley's moves wrong? "Do we actually know Charley's on Harra's books?"

"Well . . . no," Jeff said, thoughtful, "I don't reckon we do. Harra's not stupid. But if they wasn't hooked up what would the marshal be doing in Harra's office? Before breakfast, too, with their heads together and all the shades drawn? By your account they seemed pretty upset; didn't you say Longly was all set to blast you?"

It had sure looked that way, but there was things in this deal that seemed queerer than that. After all, I'd knocked him flat on his butt, called his brother a horse thief, and been in their hair at pretty near every turn. "Wonder," I said, "if Phipstadt sent for that money?"

Jeff's eyes wheeled behind the glint of

them glasses. "Why wouldn't he?"

"Everything considered, he ain't got much to gain."

Heidi stopped what she was doing to stare at me oddly. Jeff, kind of laughing, said, "Didn't you know he had his hat set for Heidi?"

Her throat fired up. You couldn't tell from her look if he was kidding or not. "I got the impression," I growled, "he was older than Moses."

The fat man laughed. "What's that got to do with it?"

I poured some more java, gulped the last of my meat. "Verdugo say anythin' about bein' over there?"

Jeff shook his head. Presently he said like it come from his bootstraps, "She ain't been back."

That brought my head up.

"No fault of yours," he growled. "Expect she's gone skallyhootin' after Charley."

There was something mighty grim in the sound of it. I remembered Heidi saying he could be pretty ruthless. She caught my look and scuffed dirt over the coals, up-ended the blackened pot and reached around for the emptied cups. "Where," I asked Jeff, "do you reckon they'll stop it?"

"Most likely place is Burnt Woman

Crossin'."

Heidi said flatly, "Red Rock!"

I stared from her to him and back again. "That's a change station, ain't it?"

Nodding, she said, "They've already used all the most likely places. They've hit Burnt Woman twice. Last time they tried the stage got away; two of them chased it better than three miles before they were able to take off the driver — they'll not want that kind of chance again. Nor won't have to at Red Rock. They can make their play while the horses are being changed."

"Too many witnesses."

"There'll be only one man at that station — old Fred."

Jeff said skeptically, "What about passengers?"

"Killing passengers hasn't ever bothered them before!"

"They're cold*blooded* enough. Probably shoot their own mothers if they got in the way," Dayne grumbled. "What I'm sayin', there's more risk."

"Risk is a gambler's stock in trade." Her glance whipped to me. "What do you think, Clint?"

I was thinking of what she'd said about passengers. From all reports these payroll jumpers never left a witness. If they'd had to chase after their quarry the last time it could only have been figured out from the tracks, and if what Jeff had said about Charley was true — The glance I pushed at him was a halfway apology. "Looks like I'll have to be votin' with Heidi."

"We guess wrong, we're stuck with it. There ain't going to be any chance to start over."

I seemed always to wind up with the women and kids. "Red Rock," I said, and his mouth twisted wryly.

"All right," he grumbled. "Heidi, you better give the kid back that rifle. We bump into that bunch he's goin' to need every bean in the cylinder."

I said, "A .45-90 is too heavy for a woman," and could see my yap didn't set none too good with him. "I'll go fetch the horses."

"No hurry about that. Be middle of the afternoon 'fore any stage out of Tucson pulls into Red Rock." It was plain he hated to give up on Burnt Woman. "It's a five hour ride right from here," Heidi said, "and I'd like to talk to Fred if we can manage it before the fireworks."

She had her way. I fetched the horses. But some six miles this side of the station her mare threw a shoe and there was no means of fixing it. Before we'd covered another three the animal was limping. By the look of the sun it was about one o'clock.

Dayne peered at his watch. "Twenty after," he said.

The heat was stifling.

Heidi chewed at her lip. "Well, there ain't no help for it, I guess," Jeff remarked, mopping at his chins. "You an' the kid are goin' to have to ride double."

It was lucky I happened to be on a stout horse. I hauled a boot from the stirrup. A wicked sound come up off the ground as Heidi stepped from her saddle. Her cheeks went gray — I reckon mine did, too. Scarcely three foot away from her a green-and-yellow tiger snake writhed into a bundle of coils, the staccato ching of its rattles holding me rooted.

Not packing no hand gun she reached for the Winchester.

"Be still!" Jeff said sharply.

The rattler's beady eyes were like translucent bits of glass. The red forked lightning of its flashing tongue went finally quiet. The snake unwound and went slithering off.

I begun to shake. Jeff was the only one with spit enough to speak. "That's the kind the Hopis use in their dances." He considered us sourly. "If you had fired that gun we might as well have gone home!"

I reached down when she come over and brought her up behind the cantle, half expecting Águila to try and get his head down, but he behaved all right, only dancing around a little, more nervous over the snake than he was of her. Someway it put me in mind of Verdugo; an odd choice of mount he was for a woman, a big strapping stallion and a speed horse besides.

He wouldn't be doing much speeding now.

We moved out at a walk, Heidi hauling her mare by the reins. We were getting into pretty rough country, about as hard to take as any I'd seen. Cracked slabs of baked granite thrust out of the earth's thin hide like bones. The pines were gone. Manzanita grew here, maguey and Spanish dagger, and the sun beat down like a brass-plated fist.

Jeff was out front now, breaking trail through this hell of rock, forced by drops to twist this way and that and sometimes, crossing places a goat would have shied at, we had to get down, blindfold the horses and walk. I guessed he knew his way around this country; if he didn't it was hard to see how we'd come out of it, such a chopped-up maze it looked to me, all cactus and stone and an occasional solitary gray-horned ocotillo lifting its naked red-tipped wands against the writhing glare of sky.

"You reckon we're lost?" I presently muttered. Heidi shook her head. "I think he's trying to find a short cut."

I didn't tell her, but a lot of queer thoughts was flopping in my head. That chase she had mentioned kept chewing on me, and Geet harping about my going to the Boll Weevil, determined it seemed to make me own up to it.

Had Longly honestly thought I'd killed Farley or was this something that had come to him secondhand from Geet? It was after the marshal had been in there yapping that Harra had told me he'd hired someone else. Yet when I'd found them together behind drawn shades there was nothing in Harra's scowling attention to suggest I'd come on things he didn't want told. I begun to wonder if I'd misjudged the man. It was Longly who'd ached to go for his shooter; and Geet, by Jeff's tell of it, was only a straw man. Charley was the killer.

Piece by piece I went over the lot, stacking things I knew against what I'd been told, trying their shapes different ways for fit, growing more and more certain there was something I'd missed. *Was it tied in some way with the marshal's brother?* Was that where the truth lay?

Something begun to move through me darkly. I'd seen nothing to prove that gangling hatchet-faced gunhawk was jumping through hoops for the camp's biggest mogul. Most of the arguments used against Harra could be applied just as forcefully to somebody else.

What if Grant's Pass Charley was doing his stuff with mirrors? Supposin' there wasn't no 'bunch' involved in these stick-ups; what if the marshal's brother was playing it solo!

But where would this leave Farley?

It had me sure enough larruping in circles. I could wish I never had heard of him even. In life he had been a card-playing shyster, dead he might be only a red herring — but he hadn't been croaked by no rattlebrained tramp. He had been done away with to shut his mouth.

I was more sure of that than I was of anything, yet it was three by Jeff's watch before the damned way of it slicked into place and left me, aghast, staring down through the windless silence into the yard of Red Rock Station.

The awful heat boiling out of that rim-locked pocket hardly touched me. The pole corrals, the paintless sand-scoured buildings starkly squatted without cover scantly two hundred yards out and down from where we stood among the gin-like smell of junipers, stacked up as less than nothing against the shock of my discovery. To put in bald words that rumbling chaos of flying thoughts requires a mind much sharper than mine. Staggered and set back I stared askance at the truth, scarce wanting to believe I could have been so blind.

"Well," Jeff said, "they haven't come yet," and, now that he'd put plain words to the picture, I could see as much for myself.

Though there was no one in sight the fresh teams were patiently standing in their harness just behind the closed gate of the day pen. And, even as I looked, Heidi urgently whispered, taking hold of my arm, "There it is!"

Where the ribbon of road came down through the bluffs a boil of dust stood against the red stone. And presently we saw the top of the stage, an Abbott-Downing mudwagon, the hatted head and hunched shoulders of the man on the box. The whip, this was. He had the seat to himself, and I wondered again if Phipstadt had kept his reported promise.

I saw Jeff's glance turn to search Heidi's face. "Somethin's wrong!" he growled.

"Where's the guard?"

"Inside?" Heidi guessed. She didn't look at me at all but went darting off toward where the horses were tied. A moment later she was back with the Winchester. "See anything yet?" she asked, breathless, of Jeff. "We better spread out a little."

He kept his eyes on the stage which now was in plain sight. "I warned you," he said. "They probably hit it at Burnt Woman."

I said, "There comes your hostler."

A feller in sun-faded jeans had stepped out of the station; at an old man's pokey saddle-cramped gait he set off to fetch up the teams from the pen. Heidi suddenly said, "That's not Fred!"

The stage was braking to swing into the yard when the man she said wasn't Fred, shoving open the gate, led out his replacements. "By God, you're right!" Jeff cried, lifting his rifle.

"Wait!" I said. "We better make sure."

But he wasn't going to wait; I could see it in his eyes.

I done the only thing I could do, whacked out with the barrel of Quail's .45-90. It took him in the muscle of that outstretched left arm. His gun went off but the shot went wild and he staggered back off balance, so furious mad he could scarcely speak.

"What's the matter with you!"

"Look —" Heidi grabbed me. I could see her mouth moving but the rest was lost in the blast of a double explosion whooming up from the yard of the station. The still-smoking tubes of a Greener were poked from a curtain of the now stopped coach and beyond it, looking more than anything like a blown-over scarecrow, was the sprawled motionless shape of the feller who wasn't Fred. "He was fixing to stick up the stage," Heidi said. "See, there's his pistol!"

Feeling kind of hung-over I sloshed my stare back at Jeff. He had his gun up again. Only now, down there, there was nobody showing for him to drive his lead at. "Where in hell is the rest of them varmints!" He sure looked confused, out of sorts and half ugly.

"Where they always been," I said, sounding bitter. "With the rest of the loose talk that's been heaved around Post Oak. You still think they stopped that coach at Burnt Woman?"

"Anyone can make a mistake," he growled, sheepish.

"You made several," I said. "Now let go of that rifle before you make another."

He gaped at me like I'd tried to kick him in the belly. "Drop it," I snarled, shaking off

Heidi's arm. "I ain't funnin' with you!"

Blowing out a great breath he let go of his shooter.

"Step outa that belt."

Like he was humoring a child the fat man done it.

"Git back away from them."

Dayne backed off, eyes rolling at Heidi. "You make any sense out of this?"

"She will," I said, "when she's had time to think a bit. And so will Mark Harra and the rest of them owners you been pointin' Charley's gun at."

"Harra," Jeff sighed. "I'm glad you dug his name from the pot — ought to show how crazy mixed-up you've got. If it's me you've picked for the brains of this outfit, how you goin' to explain *him* to Heidi? Grabbin' those claims an' bushwhackin' her daddy!"

"I been waitin' for you to get around to that. Heidi," I said, "get them stage fellas up here."

She looked from him to me. But not being one to swap broncs in midstream she set reluctantly off, pushing into the junipers, still toting the Winchester this fat crook had loaned me.

"I guess," he sneered, "you *have* come unstuck if you figure they'll walk off an' leave that specie."

Heidi heard him and paused. "Surely you didn't really think he'd send for it." She loosed a shaky laugh. "You must be even more gullible than me!"

She went on.

Dayne looked stunned. His mouth begun to tremble. "Be careful!" I said, stepping in toward him quickly. "You don't want to wind up like Charley down there!"

But he had nothing left to lose except his life; he was caught, and knew it. His arm flashed up, white hand blurring back. I hit him hard as I could with the barrel of Quail's big game gun. The knife fell out of his fist as he went down in a slanchways heap, squealing like a goddamn pig.

I said, "There ain't much doubt about where you stand *now*," and kicked all the weapons out of his reach. I stepped away from him.

Heidi come hurrying up with the driver and a rough looking oldish gent with a shotgun. Which last, with a hard sounding grunt of satisfaction, fetched his stare from the whimpering Dayne to growl, "Phipstadt here." He grabbed my paw and pumped it. "Reckon you're Farris. That varmint fit to travel?"

Jeff, moaning pitiful, dragged himself up.

"Why, you've broke his arm!" Heidi said, and I nodded.

"He tries any more tricks I'll break somethin' else. Now I'll tell you about Harra. It stands to reason he *bought* them claims. It's my idea he paid over that money and Farley, who witnessed it, tipped off Jeff. Jeff sent Grant's Pass to grab the loot and get rid of Heidi's dad. We'll prob'ly never prove it but it's the only thing that fits.

"Having got away with that, Jeff decided to throw the hooks into the rest of you big owners, and hatched up with Charley these payroll stickups. That saloon of his was the finest kind of place to start rumors. Then Farley got to nosin' around; mebbe he put the bite on Jeff. They had to get rid of him.

"Which is where I come in. Longly an' Geet tried to pin it on me. I'd broke a chair over Geet an' made him look silly. I'd knocked the marshal flat on his butt an' called his brother a horse thief in public. Both of them wanted me outa their hair. I don't think Geet had anything to do with this but Longly was tryin' to cover up for Grant's Pass. I think he must have known Charley was up to his ears in this business; he may even of known Jeff was roddin' the deal. When Geet told him I'd been over to the Boll Weevil they tried to pound a confession out of me. Longly, when that didn't work, went to Harra. Harra had hired me to fetch in a payroll.

"When I went over yesterday the marshal was with him, guess he made me out a pretty desperate character. Harra made out he'd filled the job. Longly," I scowled, swabbing sweat off my jaw, "was all wound up to take a pot at me. Just as he got himself braced to do it Verdugo walked in — girl that sings at the Weevil. Jeff had spread it around she was gone on Charley; I reckon what she was is their go-between. When she come in I busted outa there."

"How'd you come to suspect him?" asked Phipstadt.

"Passel of little things begun to add up. Remember that snake?" I said to Heidi. "You had his rifle, that Winchester he'd loaned me. 'Be still!' he yelled when you started to reach for it. He'd already mentioned your havin' the gun — seemed to want it in *my* hands. And then he didn't want to come here, kept hollerin' Burnt Woman." I said to her, grinning, "Point that gun at him now an' pull the trigger."

She looked shocked. "He's no better than Charley," I said. "Go ahead."

Phipstadt nodded. With considerable reluctance she lifted the rifle. Pointing th barrel at the sky she pulled the trigger. Nothing happened, of course. She squeezed the trigger several times. The gun wouldn't fire.

Phipstadt said, "Guess that settles it. Ought to shoot him out of hand, but he'll have his trial. A miner's court oughtn't to take much longer. You just leave him to us." He nodded to the driver, then considered me and Heidi. "No sense you two havin' to go rushing back — prob'ly got things you want to talk over." He said, kind of grinning, "There's a preacher, I heard, puttin' up at Three Pines. Just write out your depositions an' I'll take 'em on back with Dayne on the stage."

That's exactly what we done.

ABOUT THE AUTHOR

Nelson Nye is an author of Westerns who has been himself a rancher, cattle-puncher, horse-breeder, and all-around son of the real West. He's an authority on quarter horses and used to raise them on his own ranch. Now he lives in Tucson, Arizona, and does most of his riding on the keys of a typewriter. He's the book reviewer of the Tombstone *Epitaph,* and one of the guiding lights of the Western Writers of America.

Nelse has had quite a raft of good novels published under his own signature and a few pen-names as well, and is quite proud of having won the WWA Spur Award for one of them. Nelson Nye's previous Ace Book included two original novels, *Rafe* and *Hideout Mountain* (F-150).

We hope you have enjoyed this Large Print book. Other Thorndike, Wheeler, and Chivers Press Large Print books are available at your library or directly from the publishers.

For information about current and upcoming titles, please call or write, without obligation, to:

Publisher
Thorndike Press
295 Kennedy Memorial Drive
Waterville, ME 04901
Tel. (800) 223-1244

or visit our Web site at:

www.gale.com/thorndike
www.gale.com/wheeler

OR

Chivers Large Print
published by BBC Audiobooks Ltd
St James House, The Square
Lower Bristol Road
Bath BA2 3SB
England
Tel. +44(0) 800 136919
email: bbcaudiobooks@bbc.co.uk
www.bbcaudiobooks.co.uk

All our Large Print titles are designed for easy reading, and all our books are made to last.